FLY AWAY HOME

Also by Marina Warner

FLY AWAY HOME

Stories

Marina Warner

SALT

CROMER

PUBLISHED BY SALT
12 Norwich Road, Cromer, Norfolk NR27 0AX United Kingdom

Printed in Great Britain by Clays Ltd, St Ives plc

Typeset in Sabon 10/13

ISBN 978 1 78463 038 6 paperback

1 3 5 7 9 8 6 4 2

For Joanna MacGregor
And your music

CONTENTS

FLY AWAY HOME

Stories

OUT OF THE BURNING HOUSE

M Y DEAR, YOU know that burning house dilemma, when you have to choose what you would take out of it? Forget loved ones, they're thrown in, like Shakespeare and the Bible on *Desert Island Discs*. No, what would you take with you, after the wife and sprogs've been carried out of the flames in those lovely big burly firemen's arms? By the way, since when did they turn into fire-*fighters*? This gender-blind talk, on trend, not like me, like being a *chair*, or a *customer service officer* – not my style.

Making gender visible, that's more what I fancy. Adds to the gaiety of nations. We need that.

But that's by the by. As I was saying, your house is on fire, you can't fly away home, you have to decide. That artist who did long thin scribbly people – Giacometti – he said, straight off, he'd save his cat. Everything else could be done again. He was that kind of artist, he did things over and over again. But the cat was LIFE. And you can't have life over again – even if you're a cat.

He's earned lots of Brownie points from posterity for that, for choosing life over art.

But there's no doubt in my mind, much as I love moggies, and I've had a few of them over the years. I'd take my albums – as many of them as I could carry. That's why I brought them with me here, after they stopped the treatments. To my new desirable residence, Room 14 in the Ash Court Plaza, a brand-new Community Care Centre. A waiting room, an antechamber, where we sit and listen for the announcement: is your ticket number 47? The angel of death calls you and you wake up from your morphine dreams and say, Yes, Nurse, and then you're on your way through the door. Bye bye farewell auf Wiedersehen toodleloo adieu – I did think *Oh! What A Lovely War* fabulous – no more au revoir.

The knacker's yard. The Shambles. Oh, it's lovely here. Brand new, disability approved. Handles on the tub and light switches at goblin height.

We're allowed just one cupboard full of personal possessions ... I hesitated over the lovely leather toilette box I've had since that big first Xmas I played Widow Twankey at the Lyric. I used to take it with me everywhere, and the boys and girls in makeup would be miffed, but then I'd show them a trick or two, and they'd relent. Louis Vuitton, of course. No fake from Taiwan either. Straps and buckles and cleats and stuff. Big enough for one wig tucked under the fitted trays with all the eyelashes and the tubes of glue and sparkle. The Leichners all lined up, shipshape. Leichner No.6 was my standby, a lovely glow it gives you under the lights. But then I had to admit, Louie, my girl, you will never see the face in the mirror now the way it was then: photos are much kinder than reflections in the glass. So with a tear in my eye, I put the box up for auction at Bonham's in a sale of Theatrical Memorabilia, and my dear, you know what it fetched? Six months in this place. 'A classic piece of luxury baggage,' the expert said while making the estimate. It was all I could do not to say to him, Darling, I know about luxury baggage.

Anyhow in my albums you can see me from year dot. My best parts, *Spotlight* portrait shots, press releases, newspaper cuttings, programmes, the lot: that's me, there, in the picture. I can be very careful when I want to be, and I kept everything. When I was between jobs I'd buy that lovely almond paste in the tub – sniff, sniff, delicious – and put on my *Callas Highlights* and I'd ... well, the photographs were a pool and I saw myself in them, shimmering in my costumes on the gloss of the paper, the lights moulding my shape and putting life in my eyes so that, darling, I was real. There I was, the real me, the one I'd known was inside me ever since I was a titch and first saw Dame Edna on the telly.

Here I am in *Cinders*: I was Hagella, and Bobby Drew, (what a lovely girl she was!) played opposite me as Hidessa. We were outrageous, though I say so myself.

This picture here is different: it's me in the cabaret I did for my specials. Used to go round to their houses, for a birthday or some other special occasion. Specialist entertainment, can't divulge more. Some of my specials are around, you know.

Now this is something else.

I was a lad – hadn't yet discovered my inner girl – and I won the Variety Contest in the local pub. It was for imitating anyone – anyone famous. You'd call them celebs now. New Year's Eve at The Man in the Moon in Camden High Street: the Lookalike slot. It's a tradition now and they set different characters every year. Only the other day, my dear, I was the runner up in my Madonna gear: ice-cream cones for my brassiere, slinky earpiece, lots of crotch grabbing. Fabulous.

Back a bit, 1963 it was, I think, Lesley Peake was a local resident and he'd agreed to come along and judge and then – this was the real attraction – go out with the winner.

You don't remember him? He had a TV show, a kind of game show plus variety acts and a bit of talking heads stuff between him and his guests – it's become a sad old formula now but then it was new, like everything from America. 'I like to be in America, Everything free in America.' So, we're all a bit sadder now – and wiser.

Les was universally loved, as they say. Darling, he was just so beautiful. He was a beautiful man. Had eyelashes that didn't need filling out or glycerine to make them gleam and in real life when I saw him round and about our area, his stunning eyes looked like Elizabeth Taylor's – kind of violetstrokeemerald. (I can manage that look, just perfect, with the new coloured lenses.) I couldn't see that on the telly – we only had black and white then – but I studied him on the small screen and he had a way with him, the smile, the toss of the mesh of hair off the forehead, the swivel of the hips.

I was a natural and there aren't many voices I couldn't do – and I had Les to a tee, his little soft ts and ds and his round vowels still peeping through from his early life on a farm, and I could do the way he kind of semi danced forward to meet a guest and as I say, the way he tossed his hair and twinkled his eyes as he said 'Hello there!'

So at The Man in the Moon that night I had them in stitches with my impersonation.

That's me, there, doing Les, and there's Les himself.

Mirror images.

He'd agreed to go out on the town with the winner, but of course he'd hadn't bargained for … well, as I say, at fifteen I hadn't yet found my inner girl.

One of the local restaurants had donated a free candlelit dinner and the Palace had offered concert tickets – it was meant to be a Big Night Out. Plus there was the taxi fare home. We hadn't heard of men behaving badly then. No, seriously.

I begged and I pleaded with Mum to let me go … and I think the crowd in The Man in the Moon thought it was a hoot that Les Peake had to go out with a big spotty girl like me, all six bloody foot of exploding hormonal wanking calf love. But in those distant times we did what we were told by our elders and betters and we didn't go around effing and blinding like the youff of today and so it was agreed: I could have my treat if Mum came too.

This is my mum, here: she's wearing a hat she made, from rabbit skins. She had a stall in the market, Mellow Yellow Designs, floaty and dangly and chiffony. Lovely fabrics. Good at texture, my mum. A line in local T-shirts too, but she complained when the tourists started coming and she was reduced to 'I Love Camden Town' with the red heart dingbat bang in the middle. She was *creative*.

You can see here how – this is 1968 – she still has that Flower Child look, with the Botticelli hair and the little blue granny glasses. She was always a bird, even though she was my mum. 'Let a Thousand Flowers Bloom,' she'd say, when she couldn't decide what to do. 'Go with the flow.'

I took after my Dad. The nose, you know, the build. Poor little me. He was a surveyor, after his dreams of poetry were dashed by the bank manager.

I'll skip the details of that evening with Les because it all passed by in a blur. I remember going into the restaurant with Mum feeling really really terrible because I was all at odds with the outer casing that was supposed to be my body, my appearance, the way I looked. The me I knew didn't fit the me I saw in the bathroom mirror after Mum had approved my hair and my suit (broad lapels, Take Six) and my leather shoestring tie. I looked like a stranger and I didn't look like Les Peake. And I was *so* miserable about what Lesley Peake would think of me. I ordered a rum and coke like Mum – who said, no, a Bitter Lemon for you. But Les intervened, and said, Oh, let the boy have a bit of fun, go on. And Mum said, with her blue eyes rolling, Go with the flow.

That night lying on my bed not even able to get it up to have my usual bedtime you know – you're a nurse, you're not shockable – the room lurched about like in a storm at sea. It was my first time – darling – I was drunk as a skunk and madly in love.

I had it bad – you can see here, all the autograph portraits I collected of Les in his heyday.

His picture still hangs in the corridor at Broadcasting House, you know, alongside some others who've been called out of the waiting room and gone through the door. That pop star – you know, the one who died of an overdose the other day, who found out that her real father was none other than the dear old presenter of Four O'Clock Family Fun: that kind of struck a chord with me.

There's nothing like love when you've never done it before and you don't know that it will ever fade or stop. It's loony stuff, and I was loony with it: Les Peake was on my mind day and night and every minute of both and every instant of every minute and every split second of those moments squared. It was like living with a crowd of him, he filled up my head. The looniest part was that he took an interest in me: he asked after me in the pub and then he began coming round. He'd ask me to perform, and he'd laugh and laugh and give me a ten bob note or sometimes more. I began my costume collection with his help – the moolah, he called it – and I worked up acts that I thought he'd like – skits of rivals in broadcasting, numbers from the hit parade: Sandie Shaw curling her bare feet and peeping out from under her hair. That sort of thing.

He fostered my talents. He promoted me. He helped me on my way. I never would have made it without him.

Then someone in my class said to me that he'd seen my mum coming out of the Odeon on the High Street with Les one afternoon. At first, I just shrugged it off. But then I began thinking about times when Les had been round at our house and ... they say fear makes your blood run cold and that's about the way it feels. Shakespeare couldn't put it better.

The past is like a movie and I reeled the movie back: the pub, the contest, the dinner, the afternoons when I came back from school and Les would come round ... Mum laughing her head off on the sofa at my antics, fixing Les another rum and coke while Dad was watching something on the TV, reading the paper at the same time.

I went to the school office and was going to ask to use the phone, which was the only one in the building – can you believe it? – but the school secretary wasn't there. The telephone, all black and chunky, was sitting on her desk. Those were the days, when you didn't turn around and find your briefcase gone from under the barstool, when schools didn't lock up their offices. But I was scared to be there, entering without permission, and in the days when you pressed Button A in the call boxes and trunk calls went through the operator and cost the earth and mobile phones weren't heard of, ringing someone up was something. But everything in me hurt, just as physically as if I'd been run over, and I put out my hand to the receiver and dialled my mum at home and she was there and I said, 'Mum, you went to the cinema with Les.'

She didn't say, 'Oh yes, it was *Jules and Jim* and Jeanne Moreau is just fabulous or was it *The Pink Panther*? Peter Sellers is just hilarious. You could do him. You could do her.'

Or any of that sort of chatter. Not like she usually did. Of course she didn't. We weren't in the way of chatting on the phone like now.

No, she just said, 'Oh, Louie!'

And I knew, from just the way she said it.

Then her voice went all thick and she began babbling. 'There are some things, Louie, that just can't be explained or understood. It doesn't mean anything, nothing that affects you or what Les means to you and you to him. Or what Dad means to me or me to him. It's just something, darling, something that happens between a man and a woman, sometimes. You'll find the same when you're older. You'll do things you don't know why you're doing them.'

She was crying. *She* was crying. I put down the phone. When I turned round the school secretary was standing there and she was about to blast me but when she saw my face she went quiet and asked me if I needed anything.

I said no.

'Well, Louie,' she said. 'You look a bit green.'

We didn't have counselling or therapy or pastoral care or any of those things then. Les said to me, 'Think of me as your friend.'

He could charm the milk out of your tea, I'm telling you, and I would've believed anything he said. I wanted to believe him, you see.

He said I was special, that our whole family was special. My mum was a fantastic personality, he said. And he loved her.

Loving her, he said, was the same as loving me.

After that, I went on to Drama School. I extended my range.

Here I am looking drop dead gorgeous in *The Balcony* on tour – I played the Chief of Police and we took it to the Festival in Melbourne. I did love Australia.

Oh my dear, how ever does one get the kind of love one wants?

MÉLUSINE: A MERMAID TALE

Under the sea, mobile signals flutter and fail, and darling Mélusine's voice was only coming through in coughs and splutters. I do wish they'd improve our reception. It is so tiresome to have to raise your voice to a yell when you're trying to pour all your tact and diplomacy into your cowrie. But I realised that some of the interruptions were caused by Mélusine's gasps between her sobs. She loves drama, I know, but even while sighing to myself that she's still a teenager au fond, I began to be upset for her.

She was crying, 'I told him he *mustn't* ...' Then her words broke up and vanished. I waited, but nothing more came, so I said to her – or rather I trumpeted into the shellphone, 'Daarling, it isn't the end of the world. Why don't you come and see me and I'll make us a bite and we can talk ...'

'I couldn't eat a thing,' she wailed. There was a whirr and a buzz, but then her small voice returned: 'You're an angel, Morgan! I'll be there in – in this weather – less than an hour.'

Mélusine is my niece. Her mother found Arthur alone and palely loitering by a lake one winter morning during his questing days – you know the rest: she saw a lily on his brow and he shut her eyes with kisses four ... When he woke up he remembered nothing, only the bliss of it, and the unappeasable

longing that a faery encounter trails in its aftermath. Mélusine
was the result.

I was happy to be seeing her again – though she only ever
comes to see her aunt when there's a crisis – and I began gathering together some light ingredients for our supper – a crab
from my fish-pens and some samphire I'd surfaced to pick
from the dunes.

Mélusine's appetite could be coaxed, I knew.

She arrived in a new car, which didn't surprise me. She
has a tremendous flair for such things, and this one was a
vintage model she'd come across in a wrecker's yard; its previous owner – a seahorse from the Gulf, a notorious coke head
– had turned it over. Mélusine replaced the original canopy
with a giant scallop shell, harnessed six fresh young langoust-
ines in traces of seed pearls, placed two lithe mottled carp on
the rear axle, and settled herself on a cushion of sea-thrift to
drive herself at top speed to visit me and pour out her woes.
The effect was charming, utterly charming. She sprang from
the high seat before the vehicle had alighted, tossed aside the
reins to the postilions (the youngest caught them, I noted, with
an adoring look) and dashed herself against my breast with a
small and terrible cry.

Holding Mélusine in one's arms is like standing under a
waterfall on a very hot day. I stepped back, almost crushed by
the force of her passionate proximity and looked at her.

'My dear girl.' I couldn't help marvelling. 'Despair agrees
with you. I've rarely seen you look so … so splendid.'

'Oh, don't say that!' she wailed. 'You're just saying it to
make me feel better. I'm old, I'm getting to look old, which
is worse, and I want to want to be able to be my age and for

someone to cherish me in spite of it. I'm eighty next birthday, after all,' she howled.

I couldn't help snorting. That's around a hundred and fifty years younger than me, and I am still who I am, Morgan, Morgan Le Fay, and when I choose I can raise to the surface of the sea a vision of my fairy castle in the depths and mirror it on the clouds from one end of the horizon to the other. A sailor passing overhead in his ship will long only to dive down into the turquoise, then into the emerald, then into the dark purple of the sea's depths in search of my mirage. I'll draw him on and look from my kitchen range and say, as I am doing now, 'I've some nice fresh crab for supper,' and sit him down, just as I am now trying to settle the cascade of Mélusine on one of my mother-of-pearl-inlaid chairs. And I'll say, 'Welcome to my palace under the sea, wayfarer.'

Only these days I have so many other things on my mind, frankly, so many friends' lives to follow, so many repairs to oversee in my ramifying castle – though of course, when I was Mélusine's age, I didn't notice when a twig of coral was breaking loose.

She was still flowing in my arms in her torrent of grief, shaking her tumble of hair with its tangle of seaweed and little shells – she hadn't used a comb in a while, that was clear, and I reached for mine and began smoothing her head automatically, admiring the moiré glitter of her special shade of greeny gold. She quietened and pulled away from me and exclaimed, half-choked with emotion.

'Love is a complete disaster – and I'm an accident waiting to happen ...' (I couldn't help smiling.) 'I don't know why I try. I thought this time, everything would be different,' she was sobbing.

Mélusine needed no encouragement to tell me what had happened: 'You remember, darling Morgan, how it is with me: my dad, dear sweet Dad who I love and will love for ever, far more than any other man ...'

'Why, yes.' I was being patient.

'You know that the poor old thing was mortal.' I raised an eyebrow: this was hardly news to me. But Mélusine is a performer, and I was being granted a special, private performance. 'Of course you know that as a result of my special inheritance from Dad I can become mortal too – when I want.' She gave me a triumphant look. I nodded.

Personally, I have no desire to be human.

'I discovered that it's so fun – I just float in to shore, and walk up the beach a little way, and there I am, usually on the Lungomare where the townspeople are strolling and I fall in with a group of boys and girls and we have ice creams and then I borrow a bicycle or take a ride on a scooter and we'll all go dancing ... It's wicked being mortal!

'Gianni was one of our gang. He seemed different from the others, though. I wanted him to notice me. I wanted him to love me.'

I tutted at this: mermaids should act responsibly, I feel.

'I loved him, I really did – and wanted Gianni to love me back ...' Here she began crying again. 'It's not like you think, because when I'm a girl I'm not so very different from other girls, except that I don't have any family and I have to make up a story about where I come from. Gianni was suspicious, he kept asking me this, asking me that.

'One night, I decided to give him a glimpse of who I really am.'

I checked back a groan.

On certain days every month, mermaids need to take back mermaid form: like a pearl oyster in the shoals of a tidal estuary, Mélusine can survive out of her element for a while – at the very limit, from one new moon to the next. But periodically she must return to the water.

Mélusine was rushing on. 'I said to Gianni, "Come, I've something I want you to watch." I thought it would excite him, and the risk of doing it there, on land, excited me, too. I took him into our little bathroom. I kissed him on the lids once, twice, and then again, both sides, and told him to keep his eyes tight shut till I said he could open them ...

'I ran a bath and added a whole bag of salt to the water and lay down in it. Then I began humming to myself my own transformation music ...'

'Mélusine!' I couldn't help interrupting – everybody knows a mortal can't survive hearing the sirens singing. 'You didn't!'

Till now her story was like every story of a summer love affair. But now I was truly curious – had Mélusine been the death of this young man?

'First my hair sprang out in its full mane from my head, then my scales began to grow from my waist downwards, tingling me with their cool and pointed tips, and I whispered to Gianni, "You can have a peep now." My fins were pushing out from my ribs and my tail fin unfurling even fuller and glossier than before ... I was in mid-metamorphosis ...'

Mélusine stopped: she could see my dismay. I couldn't help

feeling sorry for her boyfriend, who'd done nothing except pick up a pretty girl at a party.

'Oh, Morgan,' cried Mélusine, 'don't look like that! Gianni was staring at me in the bath with his eyes bulging and making all these noises. I thought he was having a heart attack, he had such an avid look on his face. I told him he *mustn't* do that … He was scaring me, but I thought it was love, pure human craving, hot human love, the kind we mermaids don't usually know, which Gianni and I had been having all through the days and nights in our little summer apartment with the bay outside sparkling. But no …'

Mélusine dashed the tears from her eyes and blew her nose hard.

'He began laughing and leering and he said to me, "Well, two can play at that game!"'

'Bloody hell! There I was, lying all vulnerable in the bath, dreaming to myself about the sea so that I could come back in my natural shape, trusting him to see who I really am, and he meanwhile was turning himself back into whatever it is he really is – some kind of loathsome demon, with fangs and spikes and horns and things. And he was slavering …

'I'd no time to discover more. I needed every bit of my powers to magick myself back down to the sea and safe into the depths again.' She sniffed. 'It was a close-run thing. I'm telling you.' She recomposed her face and cursed furiously, then dissolved again and sobbed, 'I thought he really loved me. He's the only one I really wanted to stay with. I didn't want to come back – to this life, this aloneness under the sea where there's nothing to do, no-one to hang out with.' She checked her iShell, and shook her head sadly.

I was frowning at her, and she shot back, 'It may be all right for you down here.' She pouted. 'But I just can't get over his pretending all that time and that when I was doing my meta-morphosis – just to give him pleasure and show how much I cared – he only wanted to *eat* me.'

'Oh, darling, surely not.'

'Yes,' replied Mélusine, glumly. 'After he said to me, "Two can play at that game", do you know what he added?'

I shook my head.

'He had a nerve! He said, "Besides, I just love sushi."' She cracked a crab feeler and sucked at it vaguely. 'I do miss him – I miss Gianni, the Gianni I knew. You don't know about this kind of feeling, do you?'

I shook my head, I nodded, I shook it again – I did and I didn't after all.

I tucked her up in my best spare room, the one with the suite of mussel-shell furniture that Circe gave me for my centenary party. The next afternoon, she got up and ate a little break-fast of miso and crumbled wakame on toast, stepped up into the vintage car and turned her pale mother-of-pearl face to me, all sorrowful. Then all of a sudden she brightened. 'Oh I must show you something,' she cried out. 'It's really excel-lent!' She dived down and urged on the carp postilions to open two cigar-shaped containers on either side of the driv-er's seat. Then, with great flailings and leapings, they began to pump up bouncy balloon-like things on either side of her chariot.

'Stabilisers!' cried Mélusine with delight. 'For use in stormy weather – my own invention – you'll note they're adapted from the flotation bladder of my clever old great-grandmother!' She looked pensive for a moment. 'Darling Medusa!'

She followed the car, swimming up swiftly with strong strokes and swivelled into the driving seat and took up the reins. As she began to recede, I felt the light suddenly dimming around me, the rhythm slowing and a drop in temperature. She turned and saw me waving, and waving back sang out, 'Oh darling Auntie Morgan, you're wonderful – thank you for last night!'

I saw her disappear against the surface of the ocean and the hazy summer sky into the sparkle and glitter and streaming bubbles, and the old desire was suddenly back with a vengeance.

I would conjure again, and with the vision of my fairy palace under the sea, capture a passing sailor and bring him down to be with me and be my love.

My foolish niece is such a mischief. I never expected to have such stirrings again.

BRIGIT'S CELL

*A*NNIE *O'FLAHERTY, SCHOOLTEACHER, St Chad's, Norwich, 2011:*

– The mini-bus is stopping here because there's no parking nearer as the town centre's been pedestrianised. Then it's a short walk to Friday Market Square. It's called that because for hundreds of years the fruit, flower and veg market has happened here on Fridays ... since the days when Friday meant Freya's day ... Friday, Frigg, Freya, the Venus of the North. Anyone know the gods the other days of the week are named after?

Thor, Thursday, that's war. Yes, Jason, it's true, thunder and war. The Vikings sailed across the North Sea to this part of England, and landed here and imported their gods and goddesses. But there've been traces of human activity since the Stone Age, as well as Romans and Anglo-Saxons and Normans and, nearer our times, Dutch.

Brigit Torval, anchorite, St Bartholomew's Church, King's Lynn, 1211:

– Summer and winter sounds are as different as flowers in their seasons – as dog rose from holly, meadowsweet from yew ... They used to call me the flower maiden. They said I was made of broom and loosestrife and cornflowers and poppies ...

Annie:

– We're lucky today's Friday – it wasn't planned as the Farmer's Market only takes place once a month. The driver's going to let you off and then he'll be coming back for us – when? in two hours, and he can't wait so don't miss him! Over there are the old Hospice and Alms-houses – the Heritage Lottery Fund gave a lot of money to convert them into a Centre to bring back the past so we can all experience it as it was. To see how everything was different then. And here's the statue of the local benefactor who made a fortune and put up the fountain and the cattle troughs – why? Stephen! Why do you think he did?

Yes, good, quite right, farmers drove their stock to market then. No, they weren't any veggies then. If you were vegetarian then like you, Emma, it was because you couldn't afford to eat meat.

Anyhow this local boss generally beautified the town, which he pretty much owned lock stock and barrel.

Watch out for the traffic – market vehicles are allowed and they're a law unto themselves and I wouldn't want to lose any of you and have to tell your parents – or the school governors – that there had been a nasty accident with a white van.

Now look carefully at the wall of the church and see – there – where the brickwork changes ... no, Katie, up a bit – as high as you could reach standing on tiptoe, at that horizontal slit – it's really narrow. That's where the cell of a woman used to be. They walled her in and she lived there for ... See if you can find out how long – there's a plaque as well with her name. I'm not going to say any more. You put down your answers on your sheets – where it says 'anchorite'. I'm interested to hear what you discover … It's one of those weird stories, the kind you can't believe, but it happened, it's a real living tomb and she was a real person. They fed her through the slit that you could only reach by stretching on tiptoe. You couldn't see in and she couldn't see out.

Brigit:

– I was so sweet in perfume that honey made by the bees that sipped at me was prized above all other honey.

Annie:

– They say an owl has haunted the chimney there ever since.

No, Ben, of course it's not the same owl. Just the place has stayed a favourite haunt. Birds often go back to the same nest, you know, generation after generation.

Sometimes in the daytime you can hear an owl scuffling and shifting in its roost – they only come out at night: have any of you see one fly?

Yes, they're not exactly inner city birds: you have to come out to the country like here to find one! *(sotto voce, to herself:)* Brigit's cell really belongs in one of those stories that are old and plain and get inside your head from when your Nan used to tell them to you, the kind of stories I've always known but never seem to think about until something like this, when it involves someone who's part of real life … Nan used to mind there were so many that began with the mother dying or disappearing. 'Why for the love of God,' she'd say, 'couldn't there be more about all those fathers who do a runner? Like yours, my pet, like yours.' That's why we all came over to England – I was born soon after – all on the quiet –

Brigit:

– After I was taken to meet him, meet the man I was to be married to, we were left together in the main bedroom of his house on one of the side streets off the Friday Market. He was a merchant from Flushing, across the sea in Holland: my father had met him in the bulb trade. He was renting a pretty house with gabled windows at the back and the front, and the sunlight slanted across the floor through shutters and dappled his body – I laughed at the sight of him and he caught me up into the patch so I was dappled too.

Annie (to herself):

– I came across the plaque about Brigit on the school trip five years ago; that was the first time I'd taken Year Eight. I was standing near the wall where it says, 'The Dutch anchorite Brigit Torval retired to this cell inside the cavity wall of this church and lived here in penitence and the love of God for five years. She died aged 23 in twelve hundred and something ...' And I'm standing here thinking of Brigit's shame, during those times when you couldn't take off onto the boat for Liverpool, not like my mum ...

And I swear to God I can hear Brigit whispering to me from inside the wall.

Brigit:

– They said I was made of wild flowers, of clover and honeysuckle, dog rose and cornflowers, loosestrife and stitchwort and lady's bedstraw as well as poppies, picked in the meadows and the wildwoods, from along the edges of streams and the tangled hedgerows – and they presented me like a bouquet to the man I was to be married to, the one my father chose for me.

He was my first love – for a time we were happy, we were very happy, he could not have enough of me, sinking his face into my body. 'Oh, the scent of flowers, the flowers!' he'd say.

So I can't tell why what happened later happened or why I did what I did except that I was young and curious: was the happiness we enjoyed like the happiness of others? Did other couples feel love differently? Could *I* experience the same things in another way?

Annie:

– Have you all got your entries for the Museum? Those of you who want to, stick with me. But the rest of you can go off on your own as long as you're back, remember, at the bus at twelve o'clock. You'll know when it's time because the bells will start ringing for the daily service.

Now you've all got your sheets, so fill in as much as you can – remember there's £10 top-up on your phones donated by your long-suffering parents for the best journal kept on the trip.

You're off to find:

a stone arrowhead

the sole of a Roman sandal that was preserved in the bog outside the town

a pair of donkey baskets – creels – made from reeds cut on the marshes between here and the sea

the meaning of 'anchorite'

the name of the person who was shut up in the wall

the chimney with the owl's nest that's been there since anyone can remember ... and the kind of owl it is ... protected now because they are getting increasingly rare ...

Well, Jason, it is a bit gruesome. But it's history. It's the way some things were. We can't go through life not seeing what can happen and not caring what it is when it does. The limits of my knowledge are the limits of my world, that's something a great philosopher said. Just remember that.

So switch off those mobiles NOW – yes, I mean it – you can't take photos inside. *(To herself:)* Her merchant husband travelled across the sea, often leaving her for days at a time in his house off the Market Square, and Gerald, Count of Utrecht, came clattering down the streets one day looking to water and provision his horses, and the flower maiden fell for him, fell for him badly, with the consequences we know: the walled-up cell and the narrow window at tiptoe height.

Brigit:

– It was because of Gerald, Count of Utrecht, that I turned my face to the wall and wanted to keep to the dark and live here till all my flowers withered and my colours whitened without the sun to paint and fill them.

What Gerald made me do brought me here; what the feelings I had for him made me do. I wanted him to come to me more, more often, stay with me longer, and I resented the man I was married to even though I loved him.

Because he was there. Because he was in the way.

Gerald would send word he was coming, and then he'd fail

to come, sending word again that he had business keeping him in another place. He gave his horse more care and attention than he gave me. I envied the plate with the food he fell on so ravenously. I was jealous of his glass, too, and the way he drank from it. I wanted to be the reins he held with such grace in his hands.

Honey, the golden work of the bees. A flower maiden's closest company – they became my accomplices.

One afternoon in our garden, a swarm fastened on my husband, and stuck to him; the writhing, buzzing mass swathed him from head to foot; he flailed at them wildly at first but the poison worked quickly on his limbs and soon he couldn't struggle. They stunned him and felled his great strength like a mast cracking. No beekeeper reached him to divert the swarm; nobody came in time to lift the pulsing mass of insects from his stricken body.

I was a widow.

I was alone at last.

At first Gerald came to me and he was glad and full of wonder at my courage in this sudden bereavement. He wanted to protect me, he said. But his feelings for me weakened, I could sense it. The more I struggled to keep them aflame and strong, the more he listened to the suspicion gathering around me … and I could count our time together running down.

Annie:

– No, Emma, anchorite doesn't mean a woman who kills her husband. Anyone else have an idea what it means?

Someone who wants to stay at home?

That's not quite it, but closer … Brigit Dorval *was* anchored

24

here, so to speak, after she was walled up …

Yes, Ben, well done. Anchorite means a woman who becomes a hermit.

And why was she walled up? Katy – do you know? Yes, Sophie? Mmm, was it a way of making up for what … love … made her go and do? That's right, up to a point. But they were different times – religious beliefs were very harsh. *(To herself:)* She went to the priest here at the church on Friday Market, and confessed. He wouldn't bless her.

That hadn't changed much with the years: my mum was a wicked girl, they told her, who had led astray a good man – oh, a man like my father wouldn't have sullied his immortal soul had it not been for her wicked wiles … she should be shunned, an adulteress like her.

Brigit:

– The priest said to me, 'There is one creature – hardly made by God, though all things are – a bird all others find abominable. When it draws near, other birds rally together to cry out and warn one another. They mob it if it comes any closer, to keep it away from their children. Like you, it once committed an act of depravity for which it will not be forgiven. Like you, it must hide its shame under cover of darkness.'

He cursed me to live like an owl in the wall. He said to me: 'You will keep to the dark and all other living things will shun you. You are abhorrent to creatures of light and air, to all that is made of colour and laughter. Screeching will be your music, and others' leavings your nourishment. You will foul your own nest.'

Annie:

– Outside, I want you to talk to the stall owners and see how many of these you can identify:

tulip bulbs

iris tubers

samphire

poppies

marguerites

The local growers specialise in flowers and there's a strong connection to Holland. Which is ... where?

Yes, Emma, Holland is in Europe.

And what are the people there called? And the language?

No, not Hollandish. Anybody else? Yes, Dutch. Very good, Sophie.

Holland, also known as – anyone?

Not you, Sophie. Anyone else? No? The Netherlands. They're in fact directly east of us as the crow flies across the North Sea (which traders used to sail over, back and forth). You can see Dutch gables and other signs of Dutch culture here, like the flower trade itself.

Brigit:

– Father Damian showed me the gap between the interior and exterior brickwork of the church's structure. He wielded the trowel and left the narrow window at tiptoe height in the wall.

From the dark, my thoughts hunt for sounds stirring beyond: I can catch their quiver and tremor as you pass by and on Fridays I can hear the flower market and speak to you from my solitude.

A CHATELAINE IN THE MAKING

A FTER CLARA'S FATHER, the young corporal Gaspar Dufay, fell in the mud at Verdun with a bullet through the heart, Clara began to dance. Her mother, Eglantine Dufay, made her costumes, sometimes dressing her as a doll, or a cherry (in summer), a holly berry (at Christmas) or a pixie, and would sit watching her closely while Clara performed in cafés and bars; three years later, the little dancer was noticed by a customer, a tall gentleman in a top hat and gloves, and procured a place in the corps de ballet at the Paris Opéra. Clara became one of that select and celebrated company known as les petits rats, whom Degas has immortalised in the famous bronze, statue with her upturned face and a real tutu. In the photograph which the unfortunate Gaspar had in his pocket close to the entry point of the German bullet that killed him, the little dancer was curly-haired and chubby – consistently inspiring her first audiences to coo, 'Comme elle est adorable!' as they fixed their monocles to see her better.

By the age of nine, however, Clara had changed; she'd grown rangy, with a surprisingly long, thin neck, wrists and back, like the saluki dogs coming into fashion in that pleasure-loving decade after the First World War; in the chorus, dancing *en pointe* and wearing the flounced muslins of a *wili* or a sylph, she moved with an easy languor that belied the difficulty of the steps and arduousness of the régime. For, in spite of the hours, the rigours, and fatigue of the dancing, the Opéra became a place of safety for Clara, with allies in the company and friendly faces in the pit, where the musicians played so beautifully: the violins' sweet singing lines and the music's intricate rhythms gave her passage to an enchanted island where she could reach the grace inside her, beyond the turbulent world of the smoke-filled cafés where she had skipped and strutted as a tot.

Yet she was growing tall, taller than most of her partners in the chorus line.

The gentleman in the top hat and gloves had continued to take an interest in the little family. He was an inventor, a collector, and a designer who specialised in curiosities, which he sold to other collectors. He had a reputation as a great connoisseur. He supported Clara's mother, who was now making fans, and painting them with scenes inspired by their benefactor's taste for *chinoiserie* and other Oriental motifs. M. de Grivegarde, for this was the tall gentleman's name, backed the boutique on the rue St Honoré where she could sell her creations: *Chez Eglantine: Fabriquant – Eventails – Aigrettes – Fantaisies.*

To Clara, M. de Grivegarde was Tonton, her odd old uncle who made funny jokes and even funnier faces, and liked to show off queer things he'd found and even queerer things he'd made. He was so ancient that he had seen the Emperor Napoleon and Empress Joséphine in the flesh and even contrived for Joséphine a silver rose, of a species she cultivated in her gardens at Malmaison, which wound up and sang a serenade in the voice of the Emperor after the imperial couple had been so sadly forced to part.

On the day of Clara's fourteenth birthday, Tonton called for her at the stage door with a bouquet of white roses. Her birthday fell two days before Christmas, when it is impossible to find roses. But there he was with two dozen of them. *Petits rats* are forbidden to go out before a performance, but Tonton slipped a wad of notes to the stage door porter to sing dumb and turn a blind eye.

With her birthday so close to Christmas, there was always the danger that it might be swallowed up. Tonton was very aware of this:

'Ma petite Clara,' he'd say, '*I* shan't forget; *I*'ll make the day memorable. You are growing up now and who better than I to show you the world?'

So true to his word, he was now wishing her a very happy birthday and making a big, old-fashioned sweep of a bow, as if he might be mocking her. But she knew his weird and awkward ways, and she took the bunch of roses and dropped a stage curtsey in response.

'And I offer you my congratulations, ma petite Clara,' he went on, 'on becoming a young woman.'

They were walking together down the avenue de l'Opéra and turned left into the rue St Honoré.

'Are we going to see Maman?' she asked, as they drew near to Chez Eglantine.

'I've a different treat in store,' replied Tonton.

So Tonton was taking her out on her own; this had never happened before.

The candied fruit in Verlet's window was piled high in wooden crates for the season; Clara stopped to gaze at the café's famous spécialités, glinting with caster sugar and gleaming with waxy highlights like jades of different colours: translucent pears and luscious peaches like Japanese lanterns, frosted pineapple trapezoids, lustrous spheres of plums and mirabelles and greengages, small round star-dusted mandarins, crystallised ginger jujubes, deep-black wrinkled prunes, and scarlet and blue gleaming beads of berries like strange rosaries.

'You can have one – only *one*, mind – if you will let me have a little bite. You will, ma petite, won't you?'

Clara looked at them through the window; so gorgeous, so many, she couldn't decide. She'd tell Tonton he must decide which one; but she knew she would drink a grand chocolat au crème Chantilly, which would keep her warm inside till the end of the performance that night.

There was a bit of a queue for a table at Verlet's and they stood near the counter where M. Gérard – Tonton was exchanging pleasantries with him – was serving at the coffee grinder, scooping and measuring out the different coffee beans and fragrant tea leaves for customers' *tisanes*. Tonton was telling M. Gérard it was Clara's fourteenth birthday, and she became aware that people were looking at them inquisitively. She was used to Tonton's peculiarities when they were at home with her mother, but as she followed others' eyes in the small, crowded space of Verlet's front room, she could see why he would draw everyone's attention. He wasn't much taller than her now but he seemed vast, in his patterned and belted tweed coat à l'Ecossaise, his broad-brimmed velours hat, the gold fob watch that played a little tune every quarter, his big round spectacles, and the high stiff collar he liked to wear, which was pushed up under his jaw so that his head looked rigid, like a ventriloquist's doll's, over his frothy jabot. But here, out and alone with him, she felt conspicuous.

How to move through the packed salon de thé to their table without disturbing the other customers worried her; she wondered if she should take off her coat before she sat down, but there wasn't really room. So she kept it on, until M. de Grivegarde signalled to the waiter and bundled it with hers, and handed them both to the young man, who carried them off, giving Clara a look over his shoulder – a kind of smirk that sharpened her sense of unease. She kept tightly in her place against the wall, looking down at the foamy peak of cream in the glass in which Verlet's served their grand chocolat, and the lucent crystallised peach on a dish beside it.

'Ah, if only I could give myself such treats,' sighed Tonton, rolling his eyes at her spoon, loaded with the lovely light creamy puffcloud. 'You must eat for me and let me experience the pleasure by proxy. Youth! How you warm our creaky old bones!' Then he closed his eyes, as if suddenly in pain.

He did have such a very odd way of saying things and doing them, Clara couldn't help thinking. And she wondered how her mother felt about Tonton's funny mannerisms, his fluttering hand gestures and sudden grimaces, stretching his eyes and rolling them, then shutting them for much longer than usual.

He looked taller, sitting down, but he really was the strangest figure, Clara realised, when you saw him next to other people who were not at all like him. Out of another time, really.

Some of the company recognised who he was, she could sense it from their reactions; he was known in the sort of circles who frequented Verlet's, where the *chocolat* was the best in the city. It was his know-how that had helped spread the craze in Paris for anything and everything Oriental – for lacquered furniture and golden screens and Persian garden swing-sofas with a fringed canopy overhead; his music boxes and ornamental clocks with figurines in kimonos twirling parasols were admired by all the top collectors, or so her mother said, and her mother benefitted in her shop from the way Tonton led the vogue for chinoiserie.

Smiling at her as she tried to drink politely, he then produced a package, done up in pale blue tissue and trailing silver ribbons, and pushed in towards her, tapping it with one of his long fingernails, said, 'Here is your birthday present from me. I took advice of course from Mme Eglantine – your dear mother. You are very precious to me, and this is something precious I have made specially for you. You'll soon be a *mademoiselle*, out in the world, and when you are, you will need lots of useful things to look after you, and make sure all is as it should be. So this is a practical and useful present, even a necessity, and I hope as well that it will bring all kinds of unexpected pleasures to a very pretty young lady like you, ma petite Clara.

'Go on,' urged Tonton, still smiling. His teeth were the oldest-looking part of him, and he was usually careful not to smile so widely that he revealed them. 'Open it.'

She untied the ribbon and carefully lifted the tissue paper from a square box of elegant buff-coloured card, ruled in pale blue, with 'Fabrication Grivegarde' incised in its snug lid. Inside, nestled in a bed of mauve satin, was a cluster of silver trinkets on a hoop of silver, like a charm bracelet, but there was no slipper or a kitten or a miniature of Notre Dame or tennis racket with a pearl tennis ball, as she had seen on gifts to others among the bande of petit rats.

'It's called a chatelaine,' said Tonton, 'and it's because ...' He paused for dramatic effect and rolled his eyes in that odd way he had. 'You're no longer a little girl. You are a chatelaine in the making.'

The cluster was so brightly polished it shot lights from the box – yet it was surprisingly chunky.

Tonton lent over: 'Take it out of its box. Look at it piece by piece. Each one of the ornaments has unusual properties at your service. Secret springs and magic powers: the comb for your hair' – he picked it out from the hoop – 'will let you put up your hair in any style you like ... The key will open doors when you need to ...'

He showed her how to open the clasp that attached each of his creations to the silver hoop.

She noticed a pair of scissors made in the shape of a stork with a long beak.

'That pair of scissors will cut you the fabrics you choose in any shape you want,' murmured Tonton.

There were a dozen other devices – including a needle case with needles in it, already threaded; a thimble incised with a ring of dancing putti; and a penknife that itself opened up to reveal a fan of different instruments – a buttonhook and a pair of tweezers ...

Clara began trembling. 'Oh, oh, Tonton,' she cried. 'It is all so so pretty!'

'You'll have plenty of time to discover each and every one of these little devices,' he purred in response.

One of his creations was even odder than the rest, thought

Clara, as she picked out from the array a podgy little old man, like a wizened gnome from a picture book. When she tried to work out what it could be, she saw – she thought she saw – him give her a wink.

'By the way now,' remarked Tonton, seeing her start, 'that little toy is *the* most vital thing of all – can you guess what it does?'

Clara shook her head.

'It's a bottle stopper! It will keep the fizz in champagne fizzing for – not quite days and nights, but long enough!' Tonton was laughing and nodding. But he then stopped and grew solemn. 'I have something important to impart to you today, something more than usually important, my dear.'

Clara looked up from the strange stopper. She was excited, but also afraid. Tonton was going to tell her he was marrying Maman. This lavish birthday treat and the wonderful present were to prepare her to be happy about it. Clara knew Maman was hoping for that. Though she didn't expect to. It would be unusual for a gentleman in M. de Grivegarde's position to marry someone like Maman, Clara knew even though she could not have expressed the reasons in so many words, not exactly. But if Maman and M. de Grivegarde were married, everything would be less precarious for them. Maman had never said as much, but Clara understood that if her mother became Mme de Grivegarde she wouldn't have to please Tonton so much.

Clara felt the little man jump – could he be cutting a caper in her hand? She opened the clasp and re-attached him to the silver hoop and laid it down again in the box.

'It's amazing,' she said. 'You make such amazing things.' She tried to inject some warmth, rather than apprehension, into her voice. And she really wanted to hear what the important news was that he so wanted to impart.

'I've been collecting them for you for a while. Some I did make myself, some I came upon … here and there.'

When Clara turned over all these funny devices Tonton had attached to the hoop, they seemed to grow and to move.It was like being at the theatre, when a figure on stage, even very far away and very very small, doesn't look so tiny; you could be sitting in the gods but as you watched the stage the dancers filled the whole field of vision and could be giants. There was a miniature wheeled blade with a handle made in the shape of a woman who seemed to be laughing as she rode on the wheel, and on the penknife a hound lying along its sheath seemed to be leaping, and a miniature spoon with its shaft made in the shape of a manikin with sapphires for eyes. They twinkled at her as she looked more closely.

'Here,' said Tonton, 'let me show you something.' Leaning over, he singled out the knife from the bunch, cut a small piece from the glazed peach, and commanded it, 'Up now, up!'

The piece jumped into his mouth.

'You see – they do what you say!' cried Tonton and patted her hand. 'Wait till we get home, *petit' chérie*, and you can thank your nice kind uncle then, and give him a little kiss.' He patted his cheek. 'There's another surprise waiting for you there.'

'Are you going to marry Maman?' There, she had said it. She shouldn't have, but now it was too late.

Tonton was laughing, again. 'Ha! Something like that, yes indeed. Your dear mother Eglantine and I have been talking, and making plans. But not what you think, not those plans.

'No, first things first. You are a young lady now. You must realise that you've grown too tall – too elegant – and that the corps de ballet is no longer for you.'

Seeing her face, he waved a hand: 'You must have known. You are a swan, my dear – what shall I say? – and altogether too splendid for the chorus. You'll not be going back there. That's a relief, isn't it?

'No more stage appearances for you, *ma belle*. Instead, you'll be entering the best society. At my side.'

They took a cab back to the rue Marbeuf, where, ever since he first saw Clara dancing, she and her mother had lived together on the seventh storey, in the attic, five floors above the apartments Their single mansard window gave a glimpse over the river towards the Tour Eiffel, which was ablaze with the new electric lighting, picking out its scaffolding in golden pearls for Christmas.

They were going upstairs, Clara on edge, clutching the box with the mysterious silver baubles and her bouquet of white roses, and desperate to find her mother and ask her what all this meant. They reached the double doors to Tonton's apartment, and he ushered her ahead of him. But she held back, begging him to let her go to her room upstairs.

He shook his head. 'You have a new room now. You'll be here with me in this apartment.'

Her mother appeared in the hall.

'Maman!' cried Clara, and rushed into her arms.

Eglantine stroked her head. 'You see, *chérie*, you're entering – *we* are entering – a different stage in our lives.' Behind her, two workmen were carrying in a dressing table with a mirror across the hall into a room down the corridor. 'You will have time to get used to it. Nobody's going to force you to do anything.'

Clara clung to her mother, though she was now taller than her. She huddled, trying to make herself smaller, trying to stop this birthday from happening and plunging her into a future she had never imagined, where there would always be Tonton at her side. She wouldn't lose herself in the music of the ballet, or dance any more at the Opéra; there were to be no more *petits rats*, no more friendly violinists and percussion players sawing and drumming in the pit for the dance.

She felt a special stab at the thought of the second violin, the merry young man with his lopsided smile under a shock of black hair, who used to look up at her and give her encouraging glances and always seemed to applaud her in particular when the orchestra rose to take its bow and some of them turned to the stage to salute the dancers.

Now she would never see him again.

She wanted to bolt for it through the double doors of the apartment, down into the street or up to her old little chambre. But she also wanted to throw herself on the deep wide bed in the room they were showing her into, where some workmen were adding finishing touches to the décor and the furnishings, and which looked more luxurious than anything she had even seen, except in a picture or a stage set; she wanted to haul out the outfits hanging in the wardrobe and try on the hats her mother was pointing out to her; she was still clutching the box with the curious chatelaine and its dangling treasures. She felt panic mounting. Half-laughing, half-crying, she didn't know where to begin.

'We'll leave you to look for yourself, now, and we'll have dinner together, later.'

Her mother closed the door.

Clara looked at the room, at the fancy wallpaper, the deep soft patterned carpet, the figured curtains with silky purple tassels and fringes: against a field of bright sky blue, the colour of high summer, there were scenes of pleasure and leisure, all done in pretty Chinese costumes and scenery: a man and a woman strolling by a pagoda, and a boating party approaching an island in a river with coloured lanterns hanging on the landing stage; in the park on the island, a pair of dogs were playing together and several slender dancers trailing streamers from their outstretched hands, while a band was playing on a fancy bandstand.

Beside them, another group of merry-makers out in the park were looking up and gesturing towards a young man in an air balloon, who was sailing towards them – waving.

What was he doing there? What was he calling out as he waved?

Then Clara noticed that there was a girl below him, and the young man in the gondola of the balloon was calling out to her, and while he was waving he was letting down a rope ladder to the ground.

They had never before sat down to dinner together like this, Maman, Tonton and Clara, downstairs, in his apartment. But Clara hadn't been able to swallow down a morsel, even though Maman was very gay and bright and coaxed her. But then, when Clara said she hadn't much appetite after going to

Verlet's, Maman was annoyed, and told her not to be capricious.

Then Clara couldn't stop herself, she started to cry, and Maman became upset, she could see, because this first evening of their new life wasn't going to plan.

Tonton seemed not to mind, and told Maman not to worry, the matter could wait, he had already waited a long time.

'Are you unwell?' Maman had asked, and Clara took her chance, gratefully, and said, 'Yes, please may I leave you now?'

And Maman's voice was tight and dry when she told her to go, they would talk in the morning.

That night in her strange new grown-up bed, Clara tried to fall asleep, but her body grew hot and cold by turns; she lay rigid in the dark. She couldn't drift off for fear that Tonton on the other side of the apartment would come in, that he'd decide he'd waited long enough and Clara mustn't be allowed caprices any more.

The night dragged on, as her forebodings weighed down on her so heavily she felt she was choking. How could she escape? How could she avoid their plans for her?

As she lay there sleeplessly she thought she heard Tonton approach; she pushed herself down deeper in the bedclothes, prickling with horror.

But the sounds in the room began to take a different form, not a door handle turning or footsteps tapping closer, but a clickety-clack and a tinkle-tinkling much nearer to her, followed by murmurs and laughter.

'Shushh,' she heard. 'Less of a racket, please. We don't want to alert anyone.' Then the voice whispered, closer to her ear.

'Clara, just say the word!' The voice was like a little bell, silvery and light. 'We're yours to command. Tell us what to do!'

There was a chuckle from somewhere else, and a stifled hiss. 'You know how it is, you know how it is! "To hear is to obey" – that's what we say!'

In this strange, dark, new room a friendly hubbub was breaking out on all sides, with giggling and smothered guffaws: something from over by the wardrobe was playing the spoons while another jingling thing beside it was dancing a jig.

'We don't think it's fair. We don't think it's right. We aren't at all happy with the situation. No, no, no, no, I say. Never, never, never, we say. M. de Grivegarde! Tush, he's not the one, not for our sweet Clara, our dear Clara.' This came with a kind of skittering, like a pair of scissors.

'Tonton's old. Tonton's ugly. He should know better. He thinks he can keep ordering us about.' There were small creaks and squeaks accompanying these murmurs, as if silver joints were moving.

'And now he wants to do the same to you.'

'It's about time he knew better.'

The voices were coming nearer.

'We're fed up with him.'

'We're on your side,' one whispered.

'We know what you wish for,' hissed another.

'Strike up the music!'

'We're throwing a party! A party for you!' This voice was in her ear, lower. 'You're coming with us. To the Isle of Lanterns – this way!'

'This way!'

~

Clara sat bolt upright in her huge bed; the noises were springing up around her like the percussion section, the triangles
and the finger cymbals and the drums giving her her cue. She
peered into the dark of the curtained room, but the chinking
and clinking and cries were coming from her dressing table,
while the other sounds, the whispers and chuckles, seemed to
be coming from all around her from the walls, the curtains,
and the carpet, and even beside her on the bed.

As she looked, she felt a tug on her nightdress, and there,
standing on the bed and starting to jump up and down was the
little fat man from the champagne stopper, and he was saying,
'I can't wait to pop!'

'But you have to wait,' hissed another, shriller voice. 'Wait
till we get there – don't start now.'

'Come along, Clara! Get out of bed, it's time.'

'Hurry up, Clara, hurry up – we can't wait! We must be off
– now before day breaks.'

'To the Isle of Lanterns!'

The cries were coming all together, the tappety-tap of
dancing feet, the chinking and clinking and scurrying were
growing louder and faster, and she picked up the stopper and
turned it over and, while she was looking at it, yes, the tubby
little man winked at her again, and sprang off her hand on to
the carpet and started leaping across it like someone running
in a sack race to the window, where suddenly a shaft of light
broke in.

'Hurry up, hurry up,' came an answering tinkle from over
there, and she could see now that the scissors were dancing
with the penknife and the thimble with the buttonhook.

And they were all jumping into the boat on their way to the

island in the river and she began to pick up the music the band was playing.

'Come along, come along!' The tumult was rising.

The young man in the gondola of the balloon was waving at her. 'Clara,' he was calling out, 'Clara, this way! I'm letting down the ladder! Catch hold of it!'

She flew in her bare feet across the carpet towards the music and through the clatter and the cries.

The young man in the balloon was smiling at her – was he a friend? He certainly *looked* friendly. As she drew closer, she thought, Yes, he was familiar. Could he be the second violin? The young player with the shock of lovely black hair and the sweet lopsided smile?

Her feet were light, her head was giddy, but she felt soft little prods as she caught the rope ladder dangling from the gondola.

'Hold on tight, Clara. I'll pull you up!'

She put her foot on the first rung, and began to swing below the balloon. The sensation was exciting, like dancing. She was rising up, rung by rung, as he was making encouraging sounds to her, until she reached the rocking gondola of the air balloon and with a final last pull from the young man, tumbled into it.

He was smiling as he helped her to her feet again. Then he tossed out the ballast and the balloon began rising, drifting towards the island.

'There,' he said, 'we're off! At last – to the Island of Lanterns!'

The paper lanterns were glowing on the quayside, orange-gold pooling in the dark water, and Clara could see the party-goers already stepping out and making their way across the lawn towards the small knot of musicians who had already struck up for the dance. She could see now that some of her friends from the chorus of the petits rats were there, and the trombonist and the double bass player and the percussionist, all playing with glorious glee.

'They're all waiting for you,' said the second violinist, and he looked at her, and was serious now.

'This is the beginning,' he said, and he put his hand in hers.

RED LIGHTNING

FROM THE LOST CHRONICLE OF CENRED, KING OF MERCIA

... our pagan forebears believed, it is said, that when Hope, youngest daughter of Sky and Cloud, was turning seven, there was a party in heaven: from the four quarters of the earth, from the farthest stars and the bottom of the sea, everyone came.

But they forgot to include Hurt, their bitter cousin, in the invitation to the feast (and this was an error, and was to be the cause of much sorrow, later).

Hope's elder sister Light, who sees far away all around in the present and deep into the future, was sitting on one side of her at the table, and on her other, capricious Chance, her aunt who loves to laugh; the atmosphere was high in expectation.

Sky gave his child Hope two flints and showed her how to strike them together till the sparks flew.

She did so, and flames flashed from them like ruby suns sparkling; these dropped to earth, a precious mineral rain glowing like spun sugar, and hid in the veins of the earth. Sky then called for a pledge from all living things as a birthday gift to his youngest daughter.

Rock promised; mud, gold, silver and copper swore to keep Hope's garnets beautiful and safe. Cabbages and parsnips, clay and sand, the least of things promised their protection, too.

Sea Eagle took a pair of stones for her eyes and Swallow for her cap; the loathly Worm, too, chose some to ornament his scales.

In the towns and villages, lapidaries and jewellers, gem-cutters and goldsmiths, blacksmiths and armourers praised the new gemstones; and the short-sighted among them thanked heaven that their previous impairment was now useful, as they imagined ways of setting off the garnets' beauty.

But at the birthday party in heaven, Light, Sky's eldest daughter, eldest sister to Hope, felt a shudder pass through her. She had once dipped her finger in dragon's blood and tasted it, and so she can see everything, now and in the future, and when she picked up her cup to drink her sister's health, she saw the surface heaving to the thunder of battle and heard the clash of spears as weapon hit weapon and caerl overcame caerl and thane felled thane with swords and other weaponry glittering with the ruby gems set in gold.

She shuddered again and put down the cup and did not join the pledge.

Hope saw her and was frightened, 'What is wrong?' she asked her sister. 'Why suddenly so sad and silent?'

Light bent her head over the cup again. Warriors were tearing the bright gold from dead men, smashing and crumpling the gold and gemstones. Again, a cold shudder passed through her.

Her father, Sky, reproached her, 'Drink to your sister, Light, don't give way to your envy of the gift I made her. You have had treasure as fine as garnets and you shall have other things again, once it is your turn.'

Light tried to smile, but then her forebodings began to stir once more, for Hurt has slipped herself into the throng at the child's birthday, and in sore fury rose to curse the gemstone:

'Blood shall be the redness of the stone, and its burden to be booty in battle.'

Hurt could not work her worst: Hope called on clay and mud and grass and rock and cabbages and parsnips, on the birds and the worms to honour their promise to her on her birthday, and they gathered up all their strength to oppose Hurt's dark plots.

Yet all their power was still not enough to undo the powerful curse of Hurt, so then young Hope turned to Chance, her aunt who loves to laugh, and begged her to intervene. Capricious Chance stepped in with alacrity – crises are her meat and drink – and she laughed gaily as she promised:

'Some good shall still come of this: let the treasure sleep in a field of clay and cabbages for a thousand years – or more. And then we shall see ...'

WATERMARK

I was reading Robert Macfarlane's essay on the 'eeriness' of the English landscape and how MR James had dreamed up some queer binoculars with the gift of time travel in a story called 'A View from a Hill', and I remembered then something else about 'Monty', as he was always known. When he was still a schoolboy – he was an Eton Scholar – a new organ was being installed in the chapel, and the choir stalls and wainscoting had been taken down to make room for it. Behind them, he had a glimpse of two figures, shadowy and faint, standing on trompe l'oeil stone pedestals of curly acanthus. Their hair was loose and wavy and fanned out from their bare heads, and they were dressed in long white robes. It was an apparition: virgins in paradise!

The revelation was fleeting. Soon, the wooden screen and the stalls near and around the new instrument were put back in place and the painted figures disappeared again. But the eighteen-year-old future ghost-story writer, who was already a keen antiquarian, had travelled back in time, through the stones and plaster, wood and brass, into the Gothic chapel as it was before the Reformation, and he did not forget how, under the surface of the austere whitewashed walls, the past trembled and breathed like the landscape that seethed with ghosts when his story's protagonist put the magic binoculars to his eyes.

He was plunged into a history to which he, as an Englishman, belonged, and he found in it, not the cacophony of battle that rises from the spooky hill, but a lost grace and fantasy. Medieval Europe, lying as if at the bottom of a well, so that he would only be able to see it again if the light slanted right on the surface at a certain angle. He had seen the chapel's Catholic face, surviving when so much of the architecture, sculpture, stained glass, painting, ware and so forth of England in the medieval and early Renaissance was destroyed.

MR James was an old man composing his memoirs when he recalled the apparition, and what it meant to him comes through his words, 'I will only repeat ... that in these paintings Eton possesses a treasure which is, honestly, unrivalled in this country and in France. You must go as far as Italy (or almost as far: we must not forget Avignon) before you can find wall-paintings of equal importance and beauty.'

Gasparo Spirello was seventeen when his master, Messer Gerolamo, stopped alongside his workbench, where he was tooling a binding of the new selection of Madonna Veronica's *Canzoniere*, and beckoned him into the inner room where the workshop's books were stored before delivery to their patrons or their purchasers. Messer Gerolamo sat down at the oak table to face the young engraver, who stood before him. A *Legenda Aurea*, on which Gasparo had worked a year or so ago, lay open at the feast day of the Invention of the Holy Cross, with the woodcut of St Helena proving the true wood on which the Saviour hung by holding each of the three crosses in turn over the body of a young girl, freshly laid in her grave. Stroking and patting the great volume as if it were a favourite hound, restive and yet biddable, Messer Gerolamo, master printer to the young and clever Duchess of O——, Madonna Veronica del Licorno, looked up at his assistant and smiled.

– I have a proposal for you, Gasparotto mio, which I hope you will find an inspiration.

Messer Gerolamo prided himself on the talent he discovered and fostered, and he had known Gasparo since he was a baby – the boy's mother worked in the Castle for the workshop's attentive and most gracious patroness. For his part, the young man was relieved: when summoned, he had expected a reprimand (his execution of twining sea serpents on a colophon had been deemed skittish, and he'd been asked to quell his fancies in future).

– I am going to send you into England. *Che ne pensi, Gasparo mio?*

But the master printer did not give the lad time to reply, for he was already writing out a letter of credit, closing the huge book and thrusting it into Gasparo's arms.

– Wrap this well, giovinotto, and go home and tell your good mother to start packing. We shall be sending you there with much of our old stock. I'm putting it together – last year's prints and those from years before – in the north this is all still new to them, and they are hungry for our woodcuts. They want to feast their eyes at home on the lives of the blessed saints and the deaths of the glorious martyrs. Whereas we – and he tapped a

knowing index finger below his right eye – now have a
finer appreciation, under the aegis of our great lady.

Off with you, now. London awaits!

~

Monty was a household name when I was a child, partly because he was a friend of my grandfather's; he was Provost
when my father was sent to Eton, and it's not impossible that
the connection helped to secure him a place. Certainly, the
school inspired in him a lifelong, obsessive loyalty at a pitch
that cannot be grasped by someone who has not known an Old
Etonian, and which upset me terribly as his daughter, trying to
shape contrary hopes and ideals. Monty presided – loomed is
perhaps the better word – over the whole establishment. His
scholarly and genial presence dominated that sacred enclave,
when enthroned in the chapel, or when, his dark gown swirling, his canonicals lifting to his stride, he swept across the
school yard and stopped to exchange a few words with a boy
he knew – my father, perhaps, causing him mortification at his
gaucherie in response. In the refectory giving out the formal
grace, or at home in the Provost's elegant and princely quarters, he breathed out essence of Eton. He was a Biblical scholar; a palaeographer and archaeologist and folklorist; an inde-
fatigable cataloguer of manuscripts held by colleges and other
foundations; a loving gazetteer of churches, abbeys, cathedrals
and monasteries (their ruins). His scholarship was antiquarian, his talents hermeneutics and entertainment. In all the manuscripts he listed and annotated, he read the stories they told,
and he correlated characters and plots, proverbs and maxims

with church ornaments and furnishings that had survived the Reformers' hammers and gouges: in misericords, pew-ends, and the odd decorative elements on a grille, or placed too high up for the iconoclasts to reach.

Yet, when my father recalled him in later life, this learned and celibate figure of authority always provoked a chuckle of amused affection, because MR James's most beloved works, the writings that earned him a vast audience and are still read – and filmed – today, were his ghost stories. Gory, hair-raising, yet semi-comic, these are winter's tales in the tradition of the source books for religious frescoes, which later nourished Shakespeare's imagination, a tradition which has continued to shape current paranoid fantasy cycles about Vatican conspirators and vampire lovers. James liked to perform them on Christmas Eve by the fireside with only a candle or two to dispel total darkness.

Some of his readers have identified his hauntedness with his repressed sexuality, or his Peter Pan complex, or other Victorian particularities of his personality. His ghosts were not his alone; they are ancestral ghosts, rising from the national imaginary, filled with beliefs in relics, icons, charms, cantrips; the murky, often clammy eeriness rose like will-o'-the-wisps from fens and hills, from parish church furniture and cathedral ornaments, manuscripts and stones, soaked in his disgust with papism. The twisted morbidity mirrored his perfect state of ambivalence, as he was drawn irresistibly into through the dark backward and abysm of time.

A few years after MR James returned to Eton in 1918 in his supreme role of Provost, he began the work of uncovering the paintings that he knew had adorned the chapel of Our Lady of Eton from the era before the Reformation. The figures he had glimpsed belonged to a parade of saints, some familiar, some almost entirely forgotten in his time (the two who had appeared to him all those years ago were St Sidwell and St Winifred).

~

But Messer Gerolamo detained Gasparo to add:

– Our esteemed English counterpart and correspondent shows sharp interest in our work. He tells me the time has come for the English language – and that he's confident that our loquacious late Bishop of Genova, our revered Jacopo da Varazze of blessed memory, could become even more popular and influential than he is already with the makers of sermons and designers of church decorations – for those poor dull spirits in the north who are ignorant of Latin!

Messer Gerolamo nodded at Gasparo, for he had flinched.

– Yes, you are right. My views are no longer current, as Madonna Veronica likes to remind me. What is more, they have been out of style for a long time. It is the vulgar tongue that makes the sweetest music now!

– And our London friend does not wish to be left far behind, he writes. In his last letter to me, he declares that translation will boom in his country.

– I could send others who are older, wiser, more experienced at our trade than you. But I have chosen you from all them (he waved towards the door and the bustling workshops beyond), and Madonna Veronica agrees that you shall go. When you are there, you may keep those bright eyes of yours wide open and your clever ears pricked – and bring back news of what those ruffians are up to …

The artists who worked on the Eton frescoes remain unknown, but they were in England around 1477–87, and they dressed the figures in their frescoes in the latest stylish dress from the continent – they were scandalously fashionable as well as idolaters. Slender, elongated and fashionably dressed, dramatis personae in the miracle stories display some affinities with delicate Flemish and Burgundian journeymen's art, and a certain compositional closeness to the products of Parisian workshops, as well as similarities with other artisans in England who were making stained glass, church plate, and vestments at the time; but ultimately, they reverberate with Italian narrative verve, as found in such magnificent, complex, and vast cycles as Agnolo Gaddi's chapel in Santa Croce, Florence, and Piero della Francesca's chancel in Arezzo. There, in the 1450s, Piero painted his huge complex account of the legend of the true cross, drawing the episodes from several chapters in the *Golden Legend*, and structuring the scheme to form a total vision of Christian triumph.

The stories that the Eton artists carried with them come from the most popular works of devotion of the times – the *Speculum Historiale* by Vincent de Beauvais and the *Miracles of the Virgin* by Gautier de Coinci; but above all, the *Legenda Sanctorum (Legenda Aurea)* by the Dominican fabulist Jacopus da Voragine, Bishop of Genoa, flow into the plots. They are pictures that present the faith in a manner that was abhorrent to the Reformers who were to come within a matter of decades; the stories they tell promote typical reprehensible Catholic laxity.

They do not seem especially suited to an institution packed with adolescent boys, but they must have entertained them.

In one, the Virgin Mary is stepping in to rescue an unmarried woman from death in childbirth. In such miracles, she always intervenes to protect fallen women – and men: when a nun finds herself pregnant, Mary takes her place in the convent so that she can have the baby in peace, give the child away for adoption and then come back.

In another, an innocent Empress is raped by her brother-in-law, then accused of child murder and exiled – Mary again works to vindicate her in the eyes of all, gives her powers of healing, punishes her slanderers and brings her safely home – to another convent. Her story unfolds in eight exquisitely painted and very busy scenes; they follow the wronged heroine from persecution to triumph.

In yet another, Amoras, a wicked, dissembling youth, is making a pact with a devil and then carrying off a young innocent to be his wife; she knows nothing of his wickedness and his Bluebeard plans. But he will be foiled – by Mary.

These pictures resemble many other targets of the white-washers' buckets all over the country during the short reign of Henry's son Edward VI, and then, again, after the accession of his second daughter Elizabeth I, who issued a royal edict in 1559 that all superstitious and idolatrous images be destroyed. The doctrine of intercession, which gives Mary her indulgent role as the 'mater misericordiae, advocata nostra' (in the words of the Salve Regina), ever understanding, ever forgiving, consequently stood in the first line of attack from the

Reformers, alongside the paraphernalia of efficacious prayer – holy water, rosaries, relics. Small wonder zealous Protestants scratched out the eyes and obliterated the features of this wretched uncanonical crew of dramatis personae on the wall of Eton College chapel.

~

A struggle instantly exploded at the very core of Gasparo Spirello's being, between thrill at the thought of adventure, and horror that he was being taken from everything he knew, from O, where he had lived all his life, from his mother who would, he knew, be stricken at his departure, from his sister, Lucia, who was almost his twin in age and who also worked for Messer Gerolamo, and from his love, his darling, his angel, his robin, his thrushling, his swallow – his Fiammetta – Gasparo Spirello never could decide which of the songbirds he loved she most resembled with her quivering throat and her bright black eyes.

At the door, hugging the splendid *Legenda Aurea* to his chest and feeling the leather of its rich binding warm to his blood temperature (as if urging him to remember that even if it were now so very old-fashioned it still had blood in its veins), Gasparo turned to his master and thanked him.

As he did so, it flashed upon him that before he left he would ask Fiammetta to marry him.

~

Some of the faces of the dramatis personae in the Eton chapel frescoes were destroyed before later whitewashing covered them. These pious acts of disfigurement weren't consistent: a few female saints, a few male saints, and several characters in the stories (men and women) were obliterated like the face of the Prophet in Persian or Indian manuscripts of a similar date, when he and other Islamic saints are screened from our gaze by short veils. They are irrecoverable. The special targets of the Reformers' outrage were stories about sacred images working miracles, like the charmed mezzotint or the uncanny things – carvings, whistles – in MR James's stories: in a section of chapel wall, where a Jew is blasted for his blasphemous attack on a statue of the Virgin, her image has become a hole: in an instance of eerie duplication, the act described in the story has been repeated later by the improving iconoclast, who is ferociously rejecting in this way the hold of sacred images.

In some way, the iconoclasts of the second intense wave of the Reformation, which began when Elizabeth issued her decree, were cultural patriots; like Caxton, who successfully presented Chaucer as a new Ovid or a new Virgil in order to stake a claim that English literature could hold its own, the defacers of Catholic stories and images were asking for history to start again; they were radicals reshaping the landscape of imagination. In former hallowed ground they were hollowing a new space in which to plant another form of life.

~

... and Fiammetta said yes. But then, with a sidelong

look, the one she gave him when he knew she was going to try to get her way, she added,

– I'm coming with you. How can I let my young and beautiful husband travel alone to a country full of sad pale girls who dream of someone like you from the warm South?

Lucia was only ten months or so older than Gasparo, but she had since their father's death asserted the elder sister's authority, and she had worked long hours by day and by night, with a candle beside her (she loved the way the flame's softness brought out the gleam of the illuminations in Madonna Veronica's gorgeous coloured manuscripts) as she worked, pricking out the design of the illuminations to turn them into simple line draw-ings for Gasparino and others on Messer Gerolamo's benches to copy on wooden blocks, and when she heard that her brother was leaving for London to take a copy of the new book, she ran to find Fiammetta to share her anger and her horror, and found her future sister-in-law already trying out an assortment of her brother's clothes.

– How do I look? she asked, smoothing the hose over her thighs and laughing as she tightened the laces to flatten her chest.

Lucia flared up at the thought.

– Do you think I can let you two travel alone? she cried. What would our dear dead father think of me abandoning my responsibilities like that?

That was how three Italian youths, slender, berib-boned in silk, with varicoloured hose and velvet caps on their heads (the fashions in O were bright and witty compared to English apparel) arrived in London during the last quarter of the fifteenth century; they delivered prints from Messer Gerolamo's workshop, showed his London correspondent the several printed volumes with woodcuts they had been despatched to sell (including the magnificent folio edition of the *Legenda Aurea* with more than a hundred woodcuts, hand-coloured), and began thriving, as they reported in letters they punctually sent back home.

In the substantial glass-walled Gothic Guild chapel of the Holy Cross, Caxton's illustrated edition of the *Golden Legend* provided some other journeymen artists with patterns for the frescoes on the chancel walls, painted a few years after the book first appeared in 1483. Empress Helena was shown unearthing the Cross on which Jesus was crucified from its hiding place in Jerusalem on the Mount of Calvary. In full colour, the intrepid mission of her old age unfolded: the long journey to the Holy Land, the interrogation of the possible witnesses, the proving of the True Cross by miraculously curing a leper (in another source a young woman, recently dead), and the scattering of splinters throughout the Roman empire in order to found churches.

This fresco cycle was made for another English heartland – Stratford-upon-Avon – where the walls were also swabbed with whitewash to cover them up. The authority to go ahead and do this, agreeing to two shillings for lime pails and brushes, is signed John Shakespeare. This is William's father, who was alderman of the town in that period.

The Shakespeares' relationship to the old religion has excited much scholarly discussion. William was born around the time his father began the work of painting over the chapel's papist pictures, and the destruction continued during William's childhood, with his father presiding over the dismantling of the rood loft and the removal of the stained glass.

Catholic memories haunt the plays – sometimes literally, when Hamlet's father's ghost rises in agony out of purgatory. The family entanglement with the old religion leaves its mark on William's dramatic imagination: it surfaces in his many spectres and sinners, goddesses and virgins, and the several subjects of hallucinations and prophetic dreams. He makes a statue of a virtuous queen (Hermione in *The Winter's Tale*), and she comes to life, silently but warm to the touch at the happy end, as in a miracle story depicted at Eton. On the south side of the Chapel, the upper frieze includes one frame showing the young bridegroom who, smitten by the beauty of a statue, had promised eternal love to the Virgin; on his wedding night, she comes for him and reproaches him bitterly for forgetting his vow; she then takes him for her own, leaving his bride neglected in the nuptial bed.

That Shakespeare knew Italian has been suggested in some quarters, and even more vertiginously, that he actually was Italian! But Shakespeare does not need to have had Italian blood or known the language; his imagination is also inscribed with the shadowy watermark of the past that MR James glimpsed much later in the Chapel at Eton when he saw the shadowy saints emerge, an apparition from out of the wall.

~

Later that year, after much successful business in London, Gasparo and Fiammetta and Lucia Spirello (the two young women still successfully passing en travesti), travelled west out of London and began making their way cross country, stopping to set up shop temporarily as jobbing artists; they had held on to the remaining prints in their baggage in order to draw from them for commissions they might receive.

In Stratford-upon-Avon, where the prosperous burghers were eager to adorn their town, Fiammetta found she was having a baby; in the event, she gave birth to twins that second summer the family spent in England. This happy accident required they shed their disguises, and raised difficulties for Fiammetta and Lucia working in public. Besides, even in England, there were signs that the demand for painted lives of the saints was dwindling.

Phidias and Anastasia struck their English friends as rather unwieldy names for such tiny scraps of life, but the parents and the children's aunt took them from *The Boke of the Citie of Ladies*, where they had executed images of the artists, the sculptor at his work bench and the painter at her easel, to accompany the praises of Lady Reason.

The Spirello travellers had news from home: their great lady patroness was now celebrated for her poetry as well as her patronage. Love poetry, they were told, frank and fierce, but always decorous. All books, Messer Gerolamo reported, were now full of different kinds of feelings and different kinds of stories from the *Legenda Aurea*.

They began longing to return. They made plans to return. They began packing.

But did they?

Did the twins grow up at home, at ease with the spoken Italian of their generation? Did they meet Madonna Veronica?

Or could they have stayed on in Stratford-upon-Avon year after year, with their things half packed, expecting to leave but never quite managing it?

Or did Lucia remain behind on her own? Could she have married there?

The trail peters out.

Except for traces in the plays of their contemporary, if they can be counted evidence.

A FAMILY FRIEND

W HEN ROLLO VERREY arrived in Cairo, the name of
Ivor Whitaker was on everyone's lips. At the Turf Club, on the
verandah of Shepheard's Hotel, in the bar at Gezira Sporting
Club, in the officers' mess of the eleventh Hussars detailed to
the garrison of Lord Cromer, and in the offices of state where
Cromer ruled as Lord Protector of Egypt, the talk kept turning to the topic of the influential and wayward Mr Whitaker,
known as 'Young Whit' after his late father, even though he
was no longer in first youth.

Young Whit was still celebrated for his vigorous and
ruddy beauty, his golden hair and beard, his straight-backed
horsemanship – and his independence of thought in matters
of public interest. Rollo soon discovered that, in the highest
circles in Egypt, Mr Whitaker was often called by various
other, rather suspect names – El-Witiqui, for instance, or
the Pasha of Sheykh Omar. Rollo felt intrigued: the sheaf of
recommendations that had secured him his junior post in the
Chancery of Lord Cromer had included, he knew, a particu-
larly eloquent letter from Whit, a family friend, a confidant of
his beautiful grandmother, and a tower of strength throughout her childhood and youth of his equally admired mother,
the intrepid plant-hunter and botanical illustrator Amanda
Verrey.

Disappointment ensued in Cairo circles when Rollo could not add much to the picture of Whit himself. According to the customers of the time, an only child of busy parents, he'd seen little of them, even over the school holidays, and besides, Whit was always faraway, up to something worthwhile and heroic, even epic. Rollo had in fact only met his benefactor once. But he was such a familiar compass point in the landscape of his family that he felt he'd known him all his life.

In the city that spring, levées, luncheons, soirées, dinners, dances, suppers, even breakfasts after supper, took place in clubs and houses, pavilions and palaces, on a round that met head to tail since his duties required an early start. Rollo was meeting lots of his countrymen out in Egypt – even Lord Cromer acknowledged his existence: 'A sprog of young Verrey, and grown already? Of course you'll do. And if you don't we'll see to it.' This greeting was followed by gusts of laughter, the scented ambit of the great man richly laced with port and brandy and cigars and gun oil.

That was at a tea party: days in Cairo governing the country in partnership with the locals entailed much party going, Rollo began to see. It was at one of these gatherings that Major Crowhurst of the 11th Hussars told him of his plan to liven up the social round with some more gentlemanly pursuit than drinking tea in the afternoon. 'Cairo's deathly after a month or two – what? Nothing to be done here, dear boy. Natives ostensibly in charge, so we have to play second fiddle, dance attendance while they make a mess of things, ha, and then come after them and put it to rights – never letting on, of course. But this life is turning me soft! Before my time a lean and slipper'd pantaloon!' He struck his belly, well-corseted in his Hussar jacket.

'A spot of hunting, that's what's needed,' continued the Major.

So it was that a few weeks later, Major Crowhurst gave Rollo the job of fetching a special cargo newly arrived in Alex. Rollo would have liked to take his own horse north to meet the ship when it docked, but the cargo was to be brought later by railway to the regiment's compound in the east of Cairo. It was decided that Rollo would forgo the night ride through the desert in the cool of the dark, and travel up by train himself with his men to make sure of the preparations for the cargo's delivery.

Air and water floated overhead on the Nile delta in the hour before dawn, and in the merciful cool, Rollo made his way through the wharfs to the quay where the flanks of HMS *Shearwater* rose out of the swirl, like Gulliver tethered by a thousand tent pegs as the Lilliputians swarmed over him to pick him of everything he carried. Bundles, kegs, barrels, crates in great knotted nets swung down bulkily overhead from the gantries and, accompanied by a hullabaloo of cries, dropped into the welter of smells and sounds and colour on the docks as the *fellahin* rushed to pull them open and the quartermasters struck their ledgers and gesticulated further directions for transporting the cargo on the next leg of the journey.

Rollo's Arabic now stretched to the odd command, oath, and warning, but not much else. He plunged into the harum-scarum of the port, a path parting in front of him like the sea under a sailing ship's prow, as his men cast to right and left with their own more temperate cries and flourishes of their batons, and he had a rush to the head and the sweat prickled his neck. This was the first time he had played such a part, he, twenty-one years old, on his first detail since leaving Oxford, appointed to Lord Cromer's office and representing his Lordship's protection of Egypt. It felt something like the explosion of pleasure all over when breaking the finishing line after a race – hurdling had been his favourite sport, but he'd been a champion sprinter too.

He heard the fox hounds being disembarked before he saw them, baying loudly from the openwork crate high in the air. Neither the sea voyage nor the aerial drop quelled their energies: the pack was a squirming mass of jaws giving voice as tongues lolled, of scrabbling paws, and waving tails ... given water and meat as soon as they landed, they were penned in the shade by the freight train which was to leave for Cairo that night once it was cool again, kept for a period of quarantine and then ... the first fox-hunt ever to take place in the Egyptian desert was planned for the summer.

At night, as Rollo lay behind the mosquito veiling with the servants taking turns to fan him, the gossip he kept hearing played over and over in his head:

– Young Whit and Lady Lucy were out riding in the desert soon after they were first married, and near the old city of Heliopolis they came upon an abandoned garden – 'Sheykh Omar'.

– There's a tomb of a Sufi saint in the grounds – the place is named after him. Whit makes offerings to him, can you beat it?

– You've been there?

– Oh no, it's dreadfully hard to wangle an invitation.

– They bought the property for £200, you know.

– Not much of a pinch for them! She's rich too, you know
– in her own right.

– It was first planted by the old Khedive – Ismail – it's a
paradise by all accounts – the Khedive used to go there for
picnics. There was no house then – if they stayed overnight
they bivouacked like nomads – under the stars.

– Witiqui Pasha and Lady Lucy still do, given the chance.

– The old Khedive let it fall to rack and ruin after he himself
was bankrupted … he had bad habits, what?

– There were interested parties … we wanted him in our
grasp, don't you know?

– Whit thinks of himself as Bedouin chief, and God, he
looks the part.

– Takes their side too.

– The *Gyppos*?

– Yes. Mind you, *he*'d never call them that – to him they're
desert warriors and pure Arabians of an ancient noble race.
He's always creating about our role, saying we should get out
of the country – and give up the Canal. Doesn't see that Egypt
matters – to us. He's an 'anti-imperialist', or so he claims.
Doesn't seem to realise that it'll go to blazes without us. Or,
what's worse, to the French.

– He breeds 'osses now.

– Yes, ten years ago he began buying 'em at auction. The
finest horseflesh in all of Arabia. When Ali Pasha died, Whit
and Lady Lucy's stud farm was unsurpassed … not even King
Victor Emmanuel's could touch it.

– He breeds here now – at Sheykh Omar – a dozen brood
mares stabled there at least.

– The garden's full of wild life, but nothing like the game back home.

– Holds with some foolishness about harmony in nature if things are let well alone.

– There's a high wall all the way around the garden *and* a whole tribe of Bedouin living there as guards – they just camp there, desert-style, under tents – would you believe it?

– D'you know he turned his Arab ruffians on some Italians who were out with their guns shooting during the migration season.

– He's a law unto himself.

Laughter, marvelling laughter, harsh and bright, and much puffing on cigars and quaffing of fine wines and liquors, punctuated these exchanges.

Rollo joined in out of courtesy. Some of it he knew, though he had not heard it told in quite the same way at home.

In the withdrawing rooms where the ladies retired, in private supper rooms, in changing rooms after golf, or tennis, or a swim, these are some further things that were being said – more discreetly. Rollo was privy to much of this as well, as he found many young ladies liked to pass on what they had heard their mothers say.

– Whit did build a house in the garden to stay in.

– *Two* houses, darling girl, one for himself as Lady L's husband. The other ... well ...

– You know what he calls it – that other one?

– The Rose Villa – ooh la la. Wine and roses, don't you know?

– It doesn't end there – in private he calls it El Hashish.

– He had it built a little space apart from the main house

because ... when he has certain guests ... Lady L does *not* want them in the main house ...

– But it comes from her, you know, this fad for everything Oriental: she started him off. It was *her* idea to explore the desert, and she dresses in Arab costume too, male costume – with a dagger stuck in her belt. The pair of them, they fancy they're living in the *Arabian Nights*.

And then the informants grew softer, even more confiding. Clementina Crowhurst, the Major's daughter, imparted:

– Mummy says he has more than one family – and more than one child, the one with Lady Lucy.

– Clem, honestly, her friend Georgiana tittered.

Rollo tried to look above tittle-tattle, but his palms sweated in anticipation.

– They say after he's been ... well, the mother's friend he waits for her daughter to grow up ...

The two girls, both a little younger than Rollo, huddled their shoulders as a peal of shivery laughter shook them.

– You *know* him, said Georgie, looking at Rollo and recovering her sobriety. So you'll get invited.

– Oh, lucky old bean, that would be something! added Clem. Take me with you, oh do!

Rollo could not understand why it was that when he was in company, the figure of El-Witiqui Pasha instantly made his entrance, materialising among them as if he were at that moment streaking over the sand dunes on his Arabian mare with his wife or another in Bedouin native dress, or presiding in his floating robes over his Khedival pleasance, where ladies smoked and picnicked on carpets laid under the fruit trees and jessamine arbours, while springs filled purling pools and rilling fountains, and scents and sounds mingled with the spattered light and shade. Whit had been a figure in his family's conversations throughout his childhood, but he had never struck Rollo as quite so remarkable or indeed so peculiar before: everyone at home, especially at his grandmother's, took Whit for granted and treated every inch of him with a kind of amused admiration. Here in Cairo, it was different: underneath the hubbub of envy, curiosity and hostility, Whitaker appeared dangerous and different and infinitely glamorous, and Rollo found himself thinking with impatience of the garden of Sheykh Omar and the impending return of its pasha from England in the autumn. He also rode out into the desert to find the garden; the cotton fields running up to its high mud walls became familiar to him, but he did not enter.

A week or so later, Rollo was riding behind the pack in the hunt Major Crowhurst had mustered. They'd got up before first light and were moving west under the fading stars; his dappled mare streamed through the still pleasant cool of the early morning air. The hounds were whirling in a dense parcel of bodies, but the whippers-in were kept lively as the pack began to pick up desert scents – jackals and mongoose and a hundred other rodents. Soon, the first heat started to shimmer in the blue air and the hunt was on, racing through the cotton fields, towards the wall of Sheykh Omar; there was a stretch where it was crumbling, as Rollo knew, and he let the hounds run along the perimeter, as the huntsmen sounding their horns to urge them on. Soon they were baying from open throats after the scents they were picking up, till the point where the boundary wall was low enough for them to jump and for Rollo on his mare and Major Crowhurst on his stallion to follow the animals into the enclosure of Sheykh Omar.

The hounds made a kill, far too quickly. Their prey turned out to be a coyote. Then, wheeling round, the pack surged forwards on another wind; made a fresh kill again, almost immediately. This time, it was a fox, but a small thing, like a squirrel.

Rollo remembered the talk:

– They're his *pets* … the garden's full of animals, but nothing like our foxes back home.

As he watched the hounds at their spoil and the huntsman flick them aside and lean down to pick up the brush – which was not bushy, but sparse, he heard a cry of fury from behind him and before he could turn, a blow landed on his shoulders, and then, to a crescendo of shouts, a flurry of sticks fell on the hounds to scatter them, on the horses of his riding companions and, to his horror, on his own mare, on her neck and between her eyes.

His blood rose in rage at this assault on the animal, and he leaned to her neck to soothe her as she whinnied in fright; he struck out with his crop – all the weapons he had – to right and left, as an Arab in a none too clean djellabah seized his reins. Major Crowhurst was shouting to him to head out and was turning his own horse's head and ordering him to follow; but yet more Arabs were running up with garden tools and poles, and the affray was joined by the others from the hunt who came leaping over the wall to set about their assailants. Eventually, in the singing heat of midday, they made their way slowly back to Cairo, with three prisoners taken from Whitaker's men.

~

The repercussions of that morning sharpened Rollo's misery: Whit, alerted by telegram of the hunt and the captivity and trial of his head groom and two guards, raised the roof about the incident. He wrote to the Foreign Office, to Lord Cromer, and to the papers. He deplored the casual habits of the British in trespassing on the fields of hard-working peasants, let alone entering his own animal sanctuary. But his campaign in the public print cut deepest of all. There he expressed his surprise that more than twenty English huntsmen, with several Hussars among them, should be so frightened by a gaggle of barefoot *fellaheen* that they wailed of their wounds and thought it necessary to overpower them and throw them into the cells.

The laughter that kept rising around Rollo before the episode now became venomous to his ears. He avoided the social round as much as his post in the Chancery would allow. Then, towards the middle of September, a *suffragi*, in a blazing white turban and tunic and a red sash, delivered to him personally a letter written on heavy cream paper in a spiky cursive script.

Dear Boy,

It was a damned shame that I was gone from Sheykh Omar at the time of the unfortunate fracas. But it is my custom to return to England in the summer heat – as your beloved grandmother and mother will have told you. I did not of course know that you were of the company that my men, under strict orders in my absence to allow no trespassing, rightly drove from the garden:

my brood mares must not be disturbed, above all by any stallion in the vicinity. I regret that the subsequent wrangles involved you and caused some difficulty with your superiors. But it will all come out in the wash, I trust.

In the meantime, your mother allows me at last to meet you, to make amends for this episode that occurred through no fault of your own. So please will you join me and my Bedouin tribe, as I call my assembled friends at Sheykh Omar, this Tuesday next, 21st September, for an equinoctial ride at sundown and refreshments to follow – if you like to camp under the stars as I do, we shall make you a pillow of sand for your head. You will be very welcome.

Your dear mother brought me to you once when you were seven years old, the only time I have set eyes on you, when you were playing with your little dog and rightly more interested in her than in a foolish fond old man.

I will rejoice to see you again – salaams and blessings in the name of the compassionate, the all-merciful –

Ivor W

Rollo Verrey read the letter, and re-read it. Then he sat at his desk and began his answer. But voices kept playing in his head, and he put down his pen. Of course he longed to accept, to go to Sheykh Omar. But he would write to his mother first; he needed to hear what she had to say.

WORM WRANGLING

T HE TEPEE WAS surprisingly large; the ten or so summer camp students on the course fitted in easily around me and three other staff. The docent, a tall Indian-looking lad in jeans and buckskin shirt, a name tag identifying him as 'Jeff', and his long hair in beaded braids, waved to us to settle. There was a woven mat on the groundsheet, though the days were beginning to warm up that early summer in the Rockies. Tamar, the freckled, tightly knit Israeli girl, and Liesl, the singer from Finland who had sat down beside me the night before, folded supple limbs, tailor-wise; as did the quick-moving young man in the ragged black T-shirt with the tufted hair. With this exception, the males in the group struggled to get comfortable on the floor.

When I'm in London, I go to the Fulham public baths every Wednesday and Friday during the Third Age hour when children aren't allowed and everyone has to swim round anti-clockwise in a stately procession without showing off; when we – Maggie and me – go to the cottage in Suffolk, Maggie sets me light gardening tasks to keep me limber, and I could still tuck my feet – just – under my crossed legs on the tent floor. But I was afraid of the night's dew seeping up into my knees through the mat, as I get rheumatic stabs in the English winter. So I lost the thread as Jeff introduced himself, tapping a name label pinned to his chest. He was telling us assembled listeners about the Blackfoot nation he'd grown up with on a reservation, his grandfather talking to him only in his mother tongue. He'd first come to the city, he was saying, when he was twelve, looking for work. As he talked, he picked out exhibits one by one from a circle of baskets around him, and held them up: a bone comb, a child's embroidered and beaded and fringed chamois shirt, a spoon, a pipe. He offered them each thing reverently with his big, caressing hands; his eyes looked beyond his audience as he spoke.

The tepee was pitched between the cafeteria and the music school, on a slope planted with pines; it wore a patient air as it stood there. Around it, the contemporary glass and concrete buildings soared; farther away, the mountains made a sharp-fanged bowl of treeless granite in which the Arts Center was held. At ground level, boldly designed posters and bright flags and vivid signage set off the tent's soft painted nap and intertwined poles. As the students and visiting faculty, like me, crossed and re-crossed the looped flap of the tent on our way to the cafeteria, the faintly glowing interior seemed always to be occupied by a ghost or two, looking out forlornly.

The tall Blackfoot scooped some dark leaves from a tin, and set them alight in a pottery dish; the smoke rose. Someone sneezed, assertively.

'Smudging sweet grass,' he was saying. 'That way we show our respect for the spirits, and don't get them disturbed.' He had an accent in English, I noticed. Not Hollywood Injun; not Tonto, of course. A broad-shouldered, broad-bottomed man, I found myself thinking, with his hair in silly plaits, though.

The leaves smouldered and Jeff wafted the smoke with big

slow gestures as he snuffed it up. Some of the group followed, but one or two shifted uncomfortably and covered their faces.

The smell reminded me of the old days when journalists took you to Muriel's or to a wine bar in St James's or Mayfair, and there you could smoke – but no longer. Some young-jour-no-in-a-hurry would want to show original, imaginative zeal for the cultural health of the nation, and I, Jon Shepton, who once made an appearance in *Vogue c.* 1964 in a full-page portrait by David Bailey, would be rediscovered and wheeled on. Musician, composer, singer: I am Old Bohemia. Lunch in such places had improved no end since entry into Europe; the new chefs were young, too, sometimes absurdly well connected (the offspring of tycoon actors or footballers), and sparky, in their knotted white cravats and chimney hats. Afterwards, there were good cigars on offer. I like a small cigar, though Maggie gets cross. 'You'll ruin what's left of your voice.'

'But the fans like me rasping,' I retort. 'It's my brand.'

The guide was saying, 'We wanted to put a mark of our presence at the Center. To stop us getting forgotten.' He did not smile as he said this. 'The tepee is ...' – he stopped, and looked around the group – 'a holy symbol.'

With the others, I'd grown quiet in the tall Blackfoot's sombre presence. Though, in my heart of hearts – not very deep in my case – the smudging was just another fake from the junk shop of made-up heritage heirlooms. This is how the barren present tries to meet our hunger pangs, our craving for meaning.

Out of the blue, the people from the Center had written such an enthusiastic sensitive letter, the kind that made me feel a little bit light-headed, in spite of myself. They said they wanted to name one of the new practice cabins in the woods after me. I was a role model, 'a true artist of so many facets who's never let anyone dictate to him the boundaries of his chosen form ... The Center concentrates on fostering diversity at every level: interdisciplinary, multicultural, interactive. We would consider it a great privilege if we could use the name of someone like you. You have personified creative energy ...' It would have made me gag in the old days: official claptrap, servile and insincere – we were going to do away with all that – then. But now such recognition was rare. And coming from the other side of the world, too.

Would Jon Shepton please say yes to this tribute; please would he come? They invited me to play. Any kind of gig. That was good, they didn't think he was past it. Two thousand dollars, Canadian, and all expenses paid. Nothing more was required. Did they know that I couldn't sing as before, that the voice has gone a little threadbare and rough? But I can still growl a caustic phrase or two, especially in a small space, facing an intimate audience who love my old recordings, especially live. Plus the one or two new discs.

Now I was here, nothing much fitted with anything else. I am used to borders and seams in a familiar habitat, demarcating one area from another: in Fulham, in the council flat I've lived in for half a century, the bus lane, the bicycle lane, the pavement, the shop, the aisles, the counter; then in Suffolk, the road, the verge, the garden gate, the garden path, the threshold, the stoop, the jamb, the passage and the kilim runner. Here, in this shiny place, everything so new and the scenery around it so huge, nothing seems to have its nook, or have ever needed to find one or make a room its own. From the window seat as we came into land, I saw the dazzling spars of the city's business district, bunched together like some giant crystal hurled into the vast saw-toothed wilderness of the mountains. Rays from the low sun of the afternoon set ablaze the glass skins of the buildings. All around, brown-grey emptiness, threaded with dead straight roads pointing to the four corners of the compass, as if drawn by a mapmaker who had never set foot on the ground. The taxi that met me at the airport to drive to the Center went past oil derricks dipping their beaks into the flat wide scenery of pasture and forest; then, beyond the startling flashing and shining city, beef herds and grass. Between the oil and the meat, hovels with rusting hulks of machinery, of cars and fridges: a young woman from the reservation weaved by, thumbing a lift, lurching off the verge with her plastic bag of something, like ballast out of control.

'On the reservation,' Jeff was saying, 'there's no call for these things now.' He waved at his baskets.

In the Fifties, when I first began to play the earliest postwar night spots, improvising patter songs on the piano and telling risqué stories, the capital of this Canadian province was a small staging post on the great expanse of the middle of the country, while the town where the Arts Center grew up was one of the first mountaineering resorts. The ski lift was invented there, by some colonial genius who'd observed huge hands of bananas hoisted on board ship from the wharfs of Kingston, Jamaica, on a moving cable with dangling hooks. Or so I learned from the brochure on the town's history on the table in my room. For North Americans, the poetry of avalanches and glaciers and terminal moraines was here: no need to travel to the old world, to the Mer de Glace. In the bar of the Center, period photographs showed the tribes gathered from all over the prairies and the mountains to provide the climbers with entertainment: seamed old men with sprays of feathers and stones standing beside hourglass ladies carrying climbing tackle. This was before the boom years of beef and oil had brought the glass towers to the rocky wilderness.

Our guide was now holding up a pipe: 'When our kids get to be ten or eleven, then we teach them tobacco is holy, and their fathers will take them into the sweat lodge and teach them how to smoke, there.'

One of the students broke in: 'Hi, I'm Cindy, and Jeff, I'm kind of, well you know, disturbed. Yo'all see why, it's like very interesting, but – by the way I'm a writer, and I'm here on the ballet libretto course – don't you think that it would be better not to teach kids to smoke? I mean, it's just another problem thing for them to have to deal with – in the future, when there are no jobs and the drop-out rate is real high …'

Jeff moved his large sad head to face her, and said, 'When we lived here, before, we didn't have those problems you're talking about; and we knew when to smoke the holy tobacco and when not to. I was shown how to by my poppa. Last year, it was my turn to take my son to the sweat lodge and I taught him to respect the power of the smoke.'

'So everybody'd be just the same as everybody else? That'd be cool?'

The young man with the dark, tufted crop tilted his head and gave her a smile. 'That's what you'd like, is it, Cindy, little Miss Goody Two-Shoes!?' But there was a friendly gurgle in his voice and it cut across the scorn in what he said.

Cindy dropped her assertive look and hung her head and

muttered, with a smile under her lashes, 'Aw, you know, Adrian, you know what I mean – I mean ...'

'Quit ballet, Cindy, take up—'

'Shushh ...' Another student shut them up.

Adrian mouthed something sotto voce, and Cindy giggled and shook her head.

What was it the boy had said? 'Worm wrangling'? It couldn't be.

The atmosphere of the interior had a luminous, lulling quality: the light coming through the stretched skins reminded me of the veined alabaster set in the windows of basilicas we'd seen on a trip we made – that's George and me before, well, before he'd died – to Italy one spring.

That afternoon Brendan came to my room and asked me if I wanted to go into town with him; he's the camp's artistic director and he was picking someone up at the old resort hotel. 'It's a pile of turrets and ramparts, High Scottish Baronial Gothic,' he said, 'Definitely worth a visit. The view from the lounge over the valley is as grand as the Alps, and tea is served there with real china cups and saucers and a proper teapot with a spout that dribbles. 'You'll feel at home,' he said.

I ordered a gin and tonic.

'Make it another,' said Adrian, who'd jumped into the car with them at the last minute. The waiter came back, and I noticed he was wearing a kilt with a large ornate safety pin.

I looked at Adrian a bit more carefully. Small nose, tilted, tanned, dove's-shell-coloured eyes, a row of small teeth, and a slip of pink tongue poking behind. Body a bit meagre, but couldn't see much of it, as he was sitting. Probably older than his boyish look: early thirties.

Around us conversation puttered on, and I began to notice that they weren't coasting on automatic pilot; they were trying to be amusing, to amuse me, Adrian especially, and I was touched, and the tightness inside me eased a little. They know my work, they're pleased I'm here, I thought. And as heritage goes, the waiters' safety pins were inspired.

The following day, a walk was planned for the afternoon; Brendan was leading it, since he was a local and knew the footpaths through the mountains.

'You can just make out the mouth of the cave – look!' He pointed at a dark gravelly bluff above and facing us. 'At about two o'clock, just below the peak, can you see that mark – like a welt in the flank of the mountain? It's an ancient site, a sacred place.'

I wasn't going to try to puzzle it out in the distant rock face; my eyes watered in the clear northern light.

'It's one of the most powerful places I know in this area,' Brendan told the group. 'And it's a level climb – though it looks steep from here, it's steady going once you're on it. No cliffs, no precipices.'

When the time came to set out, I wrapped up in my lovely long camel Balenciaga from my glory days, with the brown fedora from the Italian tailor who worked round the corner in Fulham, and – at Maggie's insistence – big, ticked trainers for the mountains. The group admired my style, rather different from theirs, since they were strapped into green and brown weatherproofing and stomped about in mountain boots with water bottles hanging in slings from the small rucksacks on their backs. Adrian had oranges and

chocolate and two cokes in his; others declared their provisions in turn. They were setting off – Brendan, Adrian, Tamar
and Liesl, and Matt, a keyboard player who'd been practis-
ing in the new cabin, the one they'd called after me, and two
or three more. Then Cindy came running up, zipping her
jacket.

'I didn't know you were going this minute,' she cried. 'I
wouldn't miss this hike for anything. Gee! I'm glad I caught
you in time.'

'Oh, we thought you were ... having a nap,' said Brendan.

Cindy shook her head vigorously. 'No, I'm up and ready to
go.' She drummed her chest in gorilla play, a little strenuously,
as I realised, but only later.

At first the going was single file, along the bottom of a
ravine, up the winding dry bed of a mountain stream; slow
and difficult, between large, water-smoothed boulders over the
strew of pebbles, avoiding low scrub and thorn bushes on both
sides. The air was light, brittle, and clear; but it was warmer
between the rocks than it had been in the open space of the
Center, and the walkers tied their jackets round their waists. I
loosened the belt on my overcoat and let such small breezes as
blew in that sheltered canyon circulate around me; the broken
rhythm of the terrain was setting up a pattern and I had to
move to a tricky syncopated rhythm I rather enjoyed. But I
was being careful, and keeping an eye on my feet; the stony
ground was treacherously loose here and there. Now and then
the bed broadened, and we could walk together, two or even
three abreast; but there were always rocks to work around.
We passed pictographs on the walls of the ravine, spirals and
vertical strokes, a closed language; then before us reared a

rampart of stone, weeping with rainwater, bushy with creepers and stonecrops.

'Up there,' said Brendan. 'Look – there's the cave I wanted you to see. It's called Eye of Big Father Mountain – you can see why.'

There was a pause while the group located their goal. 'There's the track – to the side.'

The cave, from our position below it, gaped as if someone had gashed the mountain and opened a weal under its topmost pinnacle; the stuff that had spilled out of the interior core had then dribbled down the slope beneath it and dried to a swirl of caked yellowish-brown moraine, leaving the flesh of the mountainside looking tender and peeled, as if giant children had stripped a huge tree of its bark, exposing the young, pinkish cambium layer beneath.

The cave was less a mouth or a hole, though, than a kind of half-open, battered Cyclopean eye; the Indian name was spot on, I thought.

But I'd had enough mountaineering, and I sat down on a stone. Brendan gave me a waterproof something to protect my coat, and offered me some coffee from a flask. The others meanwhile set off up the scarp, calling loudly to one another. Only Cindy stayed behind with us: in her rush she'd come out in light shoes.

The climbers grew small. They were scrambling up towards the dripping eye. From where I was sitting, they looked like sinners from one of Bosch's scenes in hell, a raggle-taggle of hybrid creatures, part insect, part bird, part human, swarming into the wounds in a hollow carcass, a grotesque human ark.

Gravel shifted under the climbers' feet; a dislodged boulder bounced down the slope; tufts of dust rose as they slithered up.

'It was real dumb of me to forget my boots. I don't know what I was thinking.' Cindy laughed, then coughed. 'There's bound to be lots of bats in there. Adrian thinks bats are neat.' She paused, and added, uncertainly, 'So do I.'

A silence fell. The climbers' shouts and laughter reached us as they skirmished on the loose gravel of the slope.

Brendan said, 'Suddenly, I'm not altogether happy we're doing this ... I'm getting a kind of uneasy feeling ... I wish they'd be more careful up there.'

Cindy said, 'Low blood sugars – you need some candy.'

Brendan, nodding, took some chocolate from his bag and offered it round.

Adrian's small figure reached the bottom lid of the eye; he turned and waved as he stepped through. The two girls hung about in the entrance, and then hailed and view-hallooed us before they went in after him. Their cries trailed wide, like singing in an amphitheatre so large the sound goes out of sync with the stage.

The waiting for the group to re-emerge grew heavier, and Brendan began to make conversation.

'Oh, I do very little these days!' I replied to his question. I took another square of chocolate. 'I'm surprising myself here: it's a stimulus. One does become rather stuck in a familiar routine. Like a cat and the favourite spot on the radiator? One's own mug at breakfast – in my case, the one with the corporate arms of Weston-super-Mare. Nothing of any seriousness reaches me much any more – except when Radio

Three keeps changing the times of programmes. But none of this will mean much to you.'

With the group vanished into the cave, the disturbed ground of the slope quietened.

Looking away from the mountain, Brendan protested. He'd been at Leeds, in the Seventies, doing an M.Litt. He loved *Jazz Record Requests*.

'A very good egg, that Peter Clayton,' I said. 'That's another friend down – in his case, cancer.'

'Whoooaaargh!' The noise slammed down the rise as the climbers fell out of the mouth of the cave; one by one they exploded out of its blank eye, roaring, battering the ground with their boots and whirling their arms as they hurled themselves down the mountain, dry-skiing. The scree rose in puffs under their heels, and their cries hung for a while above in the air, like seagulls holding on to the tail of a ferry. The tracks of their flight scored deep long tears under the eye of the cave.

They flung themselves down one by one beside us. They were flushed and dusty and didn't utter, but seized on the rest of the provisions.

'It was weird in there, wild and weird.' Matt finally spoke, and shook his head. 'The silence had a kind of smell, I swear.'

'I felt I just had to get out, it was really really oppressive – and I thought the bats'd start roosting in my hair.' Liesl shook out her fair hair with her fingers. 'Yuck, I'm glad to be out of there.'

Adrian had bright spots in his cheeks. Cindy held out a water bottle and he tipped it into his open mouth.

'Any ghosts?' I asked.

'Just bats, I guess,' said Adrian, swallowing and wiping his lips. 'They stink – like old cunt.' He grinned.

Everyone began handing round snacks rather quickly at that.

Then Brendan said, as the students lay about, still panting from their flight, 'I thought I said it was a holy place. Fun and games like that aren't appropriate behaviour.'

'Oh, the natives never had any laughs, I suppose,' Adrian cut in. 'That's such a big old cliché. Granite-faced sages deeply scored by time spewing out solemn stuff about Mother Nature and Big Father Mountain.' But he was pulling off his light hooded windbreaker as he did so, and the words were harsher than the expression in his muffled voice.

'You shouldn't ...' Cindy began mocking Adrian. 'He always knows different – right? He's Mr Cool – Mr Super Cool!'

Brendan waved a hand at the view. 'These valleys were in-habited thousands of years: people moved here, survived here, with knowledge of every stone, every blade, every stream. Now we – our cowboys, our oilmen, our pioneers of the new frontier, our agro and tourist businesses – have turned the landscape to ...' – he waved at the blind eye of the cave – 'what? Desert. A mudslide, a robbed tomb, a dry-ski slope. You should – no sorry, Adrian, *we* should – show more respect.'

The speech hung; the group stared at their drinks and choc-olate, silent, uncomfortable, under the dumb blank dead eye.

Adrian at last responded. 'All I meant was that for some reason when we talk Injun talk we drop the's and a's and lower-case words and begin intoning everything in caps, to make them sound like real ancient, real primitive old-time folk. You know: Big Stick Brendan, Deep Dark Purple Sound Jon Shepton. It's a way of pushing people aside, of making history into legend and that makes it a helluva lot easier to spirit them away. Ha! At least that's how I figure it.'

'But they do have spiritual wisdom,' Liesl objected. 'That Jeff yesterday, when we were all in the tepee, he was something, he was like so still and slow and well, grand.'

'But he was teaching his kid to smoke,' Cindy cried.

'They're human beings, for Christ's sake,' interrupted Adrian. 'They're no different, hell. *No* different from you and me. Except that they don't have the bread. Or perhaps I should say, they don't have ways of getting at the bread. That's probably why Jeff has to put on this dumb kind of "I'm a wise old Native Canadian" show.'

'You should write this, Adrian, since it gets you so stirred up.' Brendan's eloquence turned from rebuking him to coaxing. 'Not that other stuff.'

'But I'm a magazine writer,' Adrian replied. 'I don't write op ed pieces for the *Globe*. I write reality colour pieces for men's mags – that's what I'm good at, and what I like doing.'

'Such as?' I asked.

The T-shirt Adrian was wearing now that he had removed his windbreaker had a logo. He tapped the sign on his chest. Then with a flourish, turned, and showed the larger legend on his back.

'I Am a Worm,' it declared.

'It's a men's movement,' said Adrian. 'It's a crusade. I joined. I am a worm, fully enrolled and paid up.

'You cry out, "Lord, I'm a Worm! Save me! Train me!"'

'And you went and did them over, of course you did.' The girl Cindy was blazing at him.

Adrian looked thoughtful. 'Hell, no, I rose in the hierarchy. I became a wrangler, a senior wrangler – I help other worms do their thing. I make a great worm. So, I got promoted.'

He paused, and through his laughter, added, 'Yeah, I do feel bad. Sometimes. I cross guys in the street and if I'm wearing the shirt, they give me a sign. "Hey man! Yeah, I'm a worm too!" But, you know, it was great.' He looked at me. 'It was so fun, you know, shouting and wailing about your sins with all these sinners.' He laughed with genuine gaiety, and I couldn't help chuckling in response.

Cindy tugged at my sleeve: 'You should read what he wrote about the sex encounter group he got into – weird stuff, really weird. Doing disgusting things to one another nobody's ever heard of.'

'Come on now, I just replied to one of those small ads that fill the back pages of papers everywhere.' Adrian's eyes were dancing. 'I'd been real curious about them for so long. Aren't you? I replied to the one that went like this: "Come free the Kundalini serpent in you!" Then in the small print: "Are you satisfying your partner? Have you developed your full sexual potential? Tantric Yoga is the key to happiness. Licensed teachers. Strictly confidential. Only couples need apply."'

'It's wild stuff,' said Cindy. 'Wild,' she repeated; on her face a scared look fought with the sarcasm. 'And he's had a ring put in his penis ...'

Adrian's head dipped, and he laughed, showing that small row of teeth: 'Now that's a story I haven't written up, so perhaps it's a rumour, eh, Cindy? Put about by certain people … ?'

She twisted her mouth and stuck out her lip at him. He didn't respond in play to her, but began gathering himself together with the others to start back down the trail.

I was walking just behind Cindy on the track when we set out for the camp. Later, when I thought back over the events of that day, the accident happened very abruptly: one moment all was fine, we were making our way in the cool of the late afternoon, with the dappled pebbles in the dry creek underfoot; the next moment, the creek was a gulf, the dry stones were knives. She was lagging behind with me and we were picking our way even more carefully on the way down, because I for one am not used to so much high-octane mountain air, and I was tired. Brendan, cheerily, was setting the pace ahead, and I felt my irritation with him begin to mount. Why had he dreamed up this difficult trek, instead of a charming stroll somewhere scenic?

But I did know why: they're pampered youth, these big kids doing summer camp studies, and Brendan wanted to put them to some kind of test.

Cindy was looking back at the weeping eye in the mountain face, and, I realised, propelling herself into a different moral position, saying something about Adrian and his sick mind when she slithered on the loose stones of the arid creek; one of them, like a flat missile in a game of ducks and drakes, skimmed across the ground under her left foot and brought her down, very hard, on her right; there was, I heard, a crack, a kind of percussive major chord, very clear, very dry.

Her face went red then white; she was instantly in terrible

pain, I could see that, and when I tried to touch her ankle just lightly, with two fingers, she flinched as if they were torturer's prods.

She couldn't speak; she was clamping her jaws tight shut not to cry out. She nodded, and her fervent eyes shone more brightly than before.

It soon became clear that some of us would have to carry her.

Adrian began carrying Cindy piggyback, as she suggested. But he soon had to set her down. So then they tried a kind of three-legged race, with Cindy hitched between Adrian on one side and Brendan on the other. She tried to hop, skip, and jump, but the dry bed of the path proved too narrow and the ground too uneven. Adrian then cut poles from saplings along the ravine with his Swiss Army knife and threaded them through the sleeves of Brendan's finest quality fleece-lined mountain climbing jacket to make a stretcher. The others took it in turns at the corners. Liesl said the army had trained her knew how to carry stuff. Every now and then they stopped and changed sides. Slowly, stumbling on the pebbles underfoot with their burden wincing in her litter at every bump and jolt, they made their way down to the Center.

I came up behind, carrying the rucksacks. I was the eldest by some way, and it was agreed that I couldn't help with Cindy and put that degree of strain on my shoulders, not the night before a gig. It proved an ordeal, just bringing up the rear with the baggage.

Later that evening, sitting with a whey-faced Brendan in the bar, I learned that Cindy had presented her ballet libretto to

the class that morning, and 'she'd been taken apart' by the others, including Adrian. Brendan shook his head over his third
bourbon and spread his hands: 'There really was little else to
say, except go back and start afresh and – think it through.
Some of these kids on computers think they can just let the
words run through their fingers and it all makes sense, because it looks nice and tidy. But Dance isn't for the birds.' He
paused, rubbed his neck muscles, and dipped his head round
and round to ease the soreness.

'They're a difficult year,' he sighed.

'How did it happen?' someone asked, coming up to the
group, flopped down in armchairs around another table in the
bar.

'He saw, he was walking next to her.' The speaker pointed
at me.

'She merely slipped on loose gravel. It's easy to do,' I said.

But the strange thing – I did not say this though – is that
after she'd fallen and was squealing with the agony of it, and
I was asking her what had happened, I glimpsed something
in her face and eyes, something wild and radiant and rather
wonderful, a kind of passion I hadn't thought her capable of.

'I wonder,' said Brendan.

'Sacred places and all that?' someone proposed, catching
his drift.

'But Cindy didn't go up there,' objected another.

'She was the most vulnerable, you know. All that negativity
– it imploded on her.'

I said nothing.

They could make out a divine plan if they chose; they could
imagine a revenge on the blasphemers. Those fellows in the

tepee were there to make them feel better about being here at all. No doubt ascribing them magic forces to turn ankles on ancestral mountain paths would soothe pangs of guilt. Make the poor buggers seem more equal in power. I drank some more to stop my tiredness feeding my hostility towards them. It's so good, I was thinking, that England is done for and we don't have to put on this silly show of respect for our forebears. In some ways, we have fallen into the past with them. At least in relation to this gleaming fountainhead of oil and gold and glass and steel. The point of it all is, I kept on thinking secretly, savagely, is that nothing adds up – it wasn't the witchiness of the place or its sacred history. It wasn't even the girl's hysteria, that blaze of fulfilment I saw for a moment in her eyes when she was in pain. Not even that. There's nothing that means anything behind the random pattern of events.

Everything is a mess: a mess brought about by chance. And by stupidity and chance mixed together, that deadly cocktail. Nothing more, nothing less.

Or is it so? There was perhaps something besides, something with genuine power, flowing between her and that young man, which shattered against him and turned back on her, making her clumsy, causing her to stumble. Yes, perhaps.

At the same moment, someone asked, 'So where's Adrian?'

'He's called it a day,' said Brendan. 'Some day. He's good friends with Cindy. It was hard on him, too, to see her hurting so hard. He felt responsible, after that class.' He bent his head to my ear, and murmured, 'I must apologise, Jon, for what turned out not at all to be the interesting and pleasant outing I'd had in mind. You've been very uncomplaining about it.'

'My dear Brendan,' I replied. 'On the contrary, I've had a most interesting time.'

Two days later, after my concert – which went as well as I could have hoped – I was leaving for the airport. When I gave my name at reception to settle the extras – telephone, mini-bar – I was handed a large brown envelope on which the name Adrian Schilling was crossed out and in the large, unpractised letters of a hand formed in the computer age, my own substituted – with the added words, 'Artist Supreme!' The receptionist smiled:

'This was left for you – Adrian said to tell you he's sorry not to see you to say goodbye, but he had to go to the hospital.' Her voice rose at the end of the phrase, as if she were making a series of proposals which needed confirmation.

There was a note inside.

Hi, Jon! It was great meeting you. You are a true hero to my generation. If you know any editors in England who might like my stuff, don't hesitate to pass it on.

Best, Adrian

PS Saw you liked the T-shirt, so, here it is (I can get another, no big deal).

The T-shirt with 'I Am a Worm' written on the back was wrapped around two magazine articles.

On the plane, I took out the one with the heading, 'Come Free Your Kundalini Serpent!' 'I'd only met Misri two weeks before,' it began. 'And every time I saw her for a date, she was so beautiful my heart jumped inside me and I felt my excitement rising hot and irresistible and melting me to the core, and I wanted more than anything to make her feel the same about me. And I didn't want to make a mess of it (I know just how bad we men can be). So we still hadn't been the whole way together when I asked her if she would like to come with me to some Tantric Yoga classes ...'

The lessons took place fully clothed, the article continued. The participants lay on the carpet in a house in the suburbs and their teacher showed them techniques. It was against the law for them to do anything, but they were encouraged to go home and practise the routines. Take it slowly, don't rush it. Explore, stroke, and tickle – all of it slowly. Take your time, the teacher said. Lots of foam baths, lots of scented oils; hand holds, caressing zones, finger insertion points, were sedulously mapped.

The results, Adrian concluded, several pages later, were terrific. Misri had nothing to complain about after they finally went the whole way, and neither did he, of course. He closed on a note of whole-hearted recommendation.

Cindy had said she thought such acts were weird. How curiously inexperienced even today's young can be, I thought, as I folded away the article and pulled the face mask over my eyes to try and get some sleep. That had been the trouble from the start of the walk, I now knew. She didn't know what she was feeling, about that Adrian. She thought he was her friend, but ... And they'd tried to leave her behind and she'd caught them and joined the walk.

I remembered the scene when Adrian was telling them about his exploits, teasing and laughing. Then I thought, Had there been time to wash the T-shirt? I felt like taking it out –

now – from my bag in the compartment above. But it could wait.

Meanwhile, as I sat in seat 25K, a soft tongue of Kundalini fire began licking at my withered core, forking through in the hardened channels of my blood. It spread, warming me through and through. Worm wrangling could wait. Instead, I could smell silvery young saliva, feel passages slippery and narrow, the intimate scrape of a nail, the yield of fleshy softnesses, hear murmurs, sighs and grunts.

AFTER THE FOX

THE HOLE APPEARED under the twisting stems of the
wisteria on the south wall of Judith's garden. It gaped too
large and too deep for a vole or a rat: Judith knew the size
of their runnels from the banks of the canal two streets away,
and when she'd had the outside lavatory at the back demolished, small neat tunnel heads soon dotted the mud where the
builder had trodden the old lawn. When she managed to call
him back again, he kicked at the holes, and asked her for emp-
ties. Taking three wine bottles from her recycling, he dropped
them into a bin liner, hammered them thoroughly till the plastic slumped like a sand bag, and then dug down into the old
waste stack and stuffed it.

'They'll not make their way up through cullet,' he said.

She remembered the word: so satisfying in its finality.

But this hole was wider than a rat hole, bigger even than a
cat flap; this visitor was no small burrower.

When Judith went out to look at her garden one morning,
hoping to find the first cyclamen uncurling their delicate heads,
she caught a panicky flash of fur and the scramble of nails on
the garden wall: an animal was writhing for a foothold on the
brickwork. When Judith stood still, the creature's first panic
subsided, and she could sense – though she could not actually
see – how the soft white fur in the hollows of the animal's

pricked ears quivered to pick up the human's response. Then, hearing no reverberating anger, the creature found its centre of gravity and levered itself on narrow, orangey haunches to vault with a squirm and a shove up and over into the next-door neighbour's garden.

A vixen, thought Judith, and a young one, too, far smaller than a spayed hearth cat, and scrawny. The hole must be a branch exit in a lattice of communications running under the gardens adjoining one another near her, in this part of the city where she'd lived all her adult life with Iain, until one morning in tears he said he'd always love her, but that now he had to care for Amanda. Judith was so resilient and proactive, she was a woman who could manage on her own. Amanda needed him more.

Since then, Judith found that to her own way of thinking, she was now widowed: death fixes memories, defaces the present, and fills every moment with the past, ablaze. His absence kept her mind in perpetual rewind – this *is* became this *was*, the time *now* the time *then*, this place *here* that place *there*, when he, when we did this and said that, ate this and saw that ... The sequence, end-stopped, the frame frozen, flickered slightly in the light of her recall. The pictures screened out everything else, beyond the possibility of change except for paling in patches, like colour prints leaching slowly of light.

This past mocked her as it flung at her, You just didn't see it, did you?

You missed the signs. You didn't know that moment was the beginning of the end and that one the continuation of that beginning and that end.

It pressed on, taunting: Iain is living with Amanda now, he

is putting his arms around her encased bones after that crash when he was driving our car, and under the plaster cast she's growing bigger with the baby she was starting to have with him all those months. For you, the past kept on, it was the last time for this and the last time for that. But you didn't see it, did you?

She was plunging through a snowstorm, flakes spinning in the darkness towards the headlights' beam and vanishing as they hit it over and over again: everything had already happened to her that was ever going to happen, and she could re-enter the sequence again at any point and it would unfold the same, a life snowbound.

So the vixen was an event, unexpected. The creature's apparition was a first new thing. She had never seen any kind of fox close up before, and she found herself wanting to see this one again: cunning little vixen, she thought. Sharp-Ears. Foxy girl. *My* fox.

She put out apples and she made peanut butter sandwiches with stale loaf after hearing a radio programme about mange. Foxes were leaving the countryside, now that fields were stripped of hedges and woodland cover and poisoned with sprayings, said an expert on a nature programme. No more hencoops and wild birds' nests – they were evolving, abandoning their traditional habitat for the spilling dustbins of the new cafés, restaurants and fast-food outlets.

At first Judith felt a twinge of annoyance – jealousy? To hear so many others talk about *their* foxes. But the feeling passed, to yield to a sense of belonging, just as, soon after her widowhood started, she found comfort in the solitude of others like herself.

'You'll adapt,' her friend Gail said. 'You'll begin to like living alone. No more short and curlies in the plug-hole.' But Judith waved away her friend: 'I'm too old for that – my mind's not wired for change, not any more. I can't pick up Chinese as if I was four years old or start balancing a basket full of stones on my head, like women building roads in India. I can't even remember the names of flowers the way I used to, and I wish the catalogues wouldn't keep changing the botanical names.'

Gail taught English at the local school, Judith Music. But in her new widowhood, when boys and girls on secondment from Biology or Media Studies came to class, she found herself scorning their utter lack of talent for the piano or the recorder, or, where it really stung the budding rock stars, for the guitar. Yet, before Iain went, she would throw herself into the school concert with relish, conducting till the players steamed. Before then as well she'd write, '*Very* promising. *Fame* calls ...' over and over again in her end-of-term reports, assuring her income. Now she had visions of slamming the lid down on a hapless aspiring musician when yet another mangled chord, rhythm, tempo, key, struck her newly sensitised ears. She began to think she must find something else to do, something solitary to suit her state.

After the fox appeared, something in her loosened and stirred and, as she'd always given advice from her work on her own patch of garden, she put a card in the local sub-post-office window, offering:

Garden Design & Maintenance
Planting Pruning Clearing Weeding Trimming
Ideas and Advice

Organic methods only.

She gave her email and a telephone number.

Soon afterwards, there was a message on her voicemail: her caller had seen the ad in the post office and needed help. 'Garden? Well, that might be the word for it ...' he began. The voice was melancholy, with the timbre of someone who might at one time have been able to sing. 'Could you come and give a quote? It'll have to be done from scratch.'

She rang the number; left a message.

That evening, the voice rang her:

'I was surprised by your call,' he said.

'Oh, why's that? You said ...'

'Yes, I know, but I didn't expect a lady gardener.'

Judith wasn't sure how to respond to this; she missed her moment as conflicting feelings arose and jeered at her for failing to choose between them – scorn of that old-style gallant condescension, and – yes – a glimmer of curiosity about someone so apparently out of sync with the times and the customs of the country. Instead she told him she worked weekends only until the holidays; the appointment was made for the following Saturday.

Sean Barbel's house stood on the lane leading to the village churchyard by the river, part of the tangled waterways that connected her part of town via the canal to his. On the Saturday morning when Judith cycled there along the towpath, the chestnut tree was tipped in auburn: a giant redhead standing and spreading limbs against the light. From the street, the house looked like a worker's cottage, with small deep-set windows in the tawny local stone, and, on both sides of the front door, grooves for a floodgate that was no longer there: so the house had been built before the canal was linked to the river to take the overspill. Which made it very old, thought Judith.

Her caller opened the front door and stood against the light from the garden at the back; turned without lingering; took her straight through, down a stone-flagged passage into a kitchen at the back, an extension from the Seventies, slatted pine and roof lights and faded druggets, and slid the garden door across. She followed him out and they stood in the first scatter of leaves under a large bedraggled cherry tree. He sighed as he kicked at the mantling weeds. As he waved – shook – his hand at the knotted thickets of ground elder, nettles, and brambles, wound around with convolvulus and dying into a sodden pile of something unrecognisable left behind by a departed builder – carpet underlay? insulating lagging? – she let a small chuckle escape her.

'It makes you laugh, does it? I suppose that's good,' he said. 'It seems a hopeless task to me. Augean stables.' He paused. 'You don't do crosswords? No, of course not.'

She bridled. 'If you're worried that a woman isn't capable ...' She stopped. 'If I'm not, I'll tell you – we might have to arrange a pick-up by the council – of the waste.' She paused, then added, 'I like digging.'

The first day, looking for tools, she found that the door to the garden shed was secured with a sturdy combination padlock. It wasn't rusty, which surprised her, as the wooden structure had grown into the damp and weedy tangle that had once been,

Judith discovered as she began to work, a hedge well-planted to deliver colour each season, with crimson-stemmed cornus, winter jasmine, dark spiky juniper and red-hipped hawthorn. The threshold was trampled and the undergrowth less dense on the approach to the locked door; the small window, with its quartered pane, was curtained; she couldn't see in.

The sodden mass by the door turned out to be bedding, and crumpled wet inside the cold matted sludge that had been a duvet, lay a nightie – with rotting lace insets round the neck-line. Judith kicked a fold of the bedding over it and a stab of ammonia rose from the mess and caught her by the throat; she clapped her hand over her mouth and nose and backed off fast.

When Sean Barbel returned that afternoon, he found Judith still hard at work, stretching her back as she contemplated with satisfaction the enormous pile of dead plants, living weeds, cuttings and prunings she had cleared.

'We'll let it settle and then, you can have a bonfire night, or, as I say, we'll call the council.' She gestured to the gunge piled by the door. 'You must have had a squatter?'

He didn't answer. He was wearing a suit and he pulled the tie loose and drew it through and rolled it in his hands, and nodded approvingly at the heap she'd made.

'Crumbs, you certainly get down to things.'

He sighed and turned, then turned back and asked her in.

Leaving her boots standing outside the back door, she asked him for the combination of the padlock.

'Oh, you don't want to go in there. If you think the garden's a mess ...'

'I thought I'd keep my stuff there – save coming through the house.' He'd shown her his garden equipment, such as it was, stowed in the broom cupboard under the stairs.

'No need.' He shook his head.

'Well, I bring most of what's necessary with me, I suppose.' It wasn't ideal, as she couldn't come on her bicycle with large tools.

'I had a wife,' he said. 'Everyone says "partner" now, but I still think of her as my wife though we weren't official, but even so. She lived here, and it's her things in the shed, you see.'

Finding a man living on his own, Judith had him down as gay; and there was something a little gay about the way he picked so carefully around his house and possessions, setting out china cups and saucers for tea. He had been russet-haired, she could see, from the silver cockatoo crest springing from his forehead where a few freckles drifted; his hands were very white as he straightened the trivet on which he'd placed a good porcelain teapot with a pattern of forget-me-nots. Looking at his fingers, she had a sudden flash: the image of these same fingers laid on her own darker flesh flickered up in her mind, weakly, hesitantly, then abated as quickly. She almost missed it, but it was something alive inside her moving, the single disturbed blade that tells the tracker something has passed this way.

The second week she was working on his garden, he returned in the early evening and asked her, with stiff good manners, if she liked going to bed with men, and if so, would she consider going to bed with him? He did not add anything more.

He was standing near her in the garden where she was still hoeing by the light of a big lamp she'd looped over a branch.

Judith told him she was out of practice; then, gesturing at her state, asked if she might use the shower first. He gave her a towel, and then, calling through the door, offered her a dressing gown. She kept her mind on not slipping, not splashing too much, and cleansed herself with a cat's assiduity. No, she was not going to think of the possible condition of Sean's bed.

The dressing gown was silky, with embroidered panels, Chinese. When she came out he didn't say anything to her as he busied around her barely dried form. He was eager; she found herself surprised: a feeling of festivity, a flash over her limbs. He patted her and said, 'You don't seem to have forgotten how to do it.' He laughed then, and added, 'I have to say, I thought I had.'

Back in her own house, Judith went out into her own garden and put down food for her fox; she wanted the animal to be there, for though her sleeping with Sean had surprised her, it didn't lift the solitude.

On the radiator shelf in the hall at Sean Barbel's cottage, there some piles of small change, a few old business cards, drawing pins and paper clips and rubber bands from postmen's bundles, peppermints and receipts accumulated in various chipped saucers; also, keys. Sean showed her how they were tagged to identify them: cellar, garden door, side door, front-room window locks; and a slip of crumpled paper with 'garden shed' written in felt tip, and a number. She did not mean to take it in, but the digits impressed themselves as if they had spoken aloud.

She was making a rockery on the south-westerly slope at

the end of the garden, where she'd collected together the old bricks and rocks she'd dug up in the rest of the plot, and as she worked, her back was to the garden shed with its mute door and small blind window with the gingham curtain tucked against it on the inside and the combination lock on the hasp across the entrance. But she felt its presence behind her; one afternoon she peeped in again through the gap where the curtain, on its wire, sagged in the centre of the window, and saw that a postcard which she felt sure hadn't been there before was propped up against the pane, its picture side turned inwards, the message and the address legible on her side of the glass. It was addressed to Daisy Sulter, and came from Turkey; the caption identified the image, as 'Suleimanye mosque. Beautiful worship place'. It was old, postmarked something something 197-something, as far as she could decipher it. The message read,

> Conference boring but have played truant and tried to find the carpet shop where we bought ours – they all looked the same and when I asked, two merchants at least fell on me like an old friend. Need your eye, but shan't say wish you were here,
> Love, Sean.
> PS Back before this reaches you, probably!

Judith revolved the cogs on the padlock to the number still clear in her head; the interior was in shadow, and she took a moment or two to see what the garden shed held. It was full of stuff, as Sean had warned. But whereas Judith had expected a stack of tea chests, and perhaps a shelf of rusting antifreeze and some hardened sacks of fertiliser, she found she was looking at a tiny, neat bedroom.

The shed was a Wendy house, with a narrow, low bed, tucked in and covered by a satin eiderdown stitched in a floral design; one pillow set straight; a low cupboard, doubling as a bedside table; a pair of chemist's reading glasses lying there, next to a china ewer and basin with cabbage roses; on the floor, a round tatting mat, variegated, and a pair of Wellingtons with mud on them; hanging on a hook beside the window, the slippery silk dressing gown, Chinese sprays of embroidery on glowing crimson panels.

Judith drew back, slid the hinge of the lock and lifted the hasp with fluttering fingers, her heart pumping blood to her temples.

'Daisy turned against me, for some reason she wouldn't give,' Sean explained under some constraint the following week. He resisted Judith's attempts to turn over the past. 'Perhaps she didn't know it herself.'

'But ...' Judith wanted to object, but fell silent, not to give away her trespassing.

'I could see I irritated her,' Sean went on, 'that my very presence set her teeth on edge, that my touch repelled her.' He sighed and turned towards Judith, and put a fingertip to her shoulder above her breast. 'You are different, you see. You rather like sex. At least you seem to – with me.

'I used to think she had a lover, someone else,' he said. 'Though she wouldn't ever admit it. So one night, after a terrible time, when she rejected me and said she would never sleep with me again, I rushed out into the garden and went to sleep in the shed. After that, it became a kind of habit – injured pride, that kind of thing. Then one thing led to another – you know the rest.'

Judith didn't; except that Daisy, his first wife, had left him eight years ago, and that afterwards there had been a potter called Sylvie.

'I don't know why,' he said, again.

She tucked herself closer in to his body, thinking of the garden shed. His limbs, in which something had leaped a short while ago, now felt damp and chill.

'Then, after Daisy moved out, she sometimes came back without warning. She still had keys. Once she arrived when I was ... Well.' He turned on to his back and lifted himself up the bed a little to laugh. 'Her appearance for all intents and purposes as if she still lived here ... it did not please my guest, as you can imagine. But as for Daisy, she didn't turn a hair.'

'Who was that?'

'Meriel, that was her name. Pretty. Her name, I mean. She was only middling good-looking. But a fine viola player. We played together in the quartet I ...'

Now there were too many paths: the memory map was lifting into new land masses, trackless wastes, and new creatures of unknown feature and behaviour were roaming its unknown expanses.

Judith ignored Meriel for the time being. For now, she'd keep to another track:

'Where is she now? Sylvie?'

There was a pause.

'North Carolina, she has a husband there – she met him through one of her courses. She liked taking courses: Buddhism one year, caning another.' He laughed. 'Basketwork. Not the other sort. A broker husband. And children. She doesn't write. Of all the women … Ouch.' He broke off, as Judith pinched him. 'Well, we're not so young that we have to pretend, surely – she is the one I've most lost contact with.' He turned Judith's face with his hands to look at her. 'I'm being tactless.' It was his turn to pinch her, gently. 'Aren't you speaking to me any more?'

Every time Judith turned over something she'd retrieved from the past life Sean had lived in the house and its over-grown garden, it slipped and changed, as certain flowers under sodium street lamps turn sulphurous, an elegant pale yellow becoming dirty dishwater, and crimson blossom reddish-brown scuzz.

One afternoon, when Judith had let herself in to the house and was walking through into the garden, Meriel was sitting at the kitchen table warming her hands on the teapot. Judith could not mistake her, in the velour hat she'd seen from one of Sean's photograph, with her curling dark 'pre-Raphaelite hair' spill-ing out under it: she looked as she must have looked when they were together, thought Judith. An aroma of citrus and vanilla emanated from her pale skin and large, sad, ringed eyes.

She began talking about Sean to Judith without a pause, warmly, kindly, like a big sister who has learned that the youngest in the family has found a boyfriend for the first time.

'Don't you find yourself feeling sorry for him? Because he seems so cast down by life? I know I do. Still, after all these years.

'I hope he's paying you properly. He can be very vague about that kind of thing, and when you're sleeping with him, it's sometimes a bit sensitive to ask for money.' (At this she giggled.) 'It's not his way, that, not at all. He may be hopelessly, chronically, congenitally unable to be faithful to one woman, but he would feel utterly defeated if he had to shell out for it.'

She took a sip of tea and looked up at Judith, her soft eyes moist with mischief:

'Has he peed in front of you yet? He loves that. Just a little boy at heart.' She laughed. 'With a big whoosh. Oh, intimacy with Sean is a game, just a game.' She pushed a cup towards Judith and began pouring.

'And has he twisted you round yet when you're having sex? So you're upside down on top of him? He thinks that's awfully clever.'

Later, making her way downstairs, she saw the door to the side of the main bedroom was ajar. It led to a kind of glory hole, where Sean tossed things he didn't want to throw away. She pushed it open and looked inside. Flung on the chair was a skirt, a good, shapely skirt, made of some kind of soft wool in a deep maroon brown. She was magnetised by it, plucked it from its place; it was warm to the touch, and wafted a scent of something alive as she lifted it. The skirt filled as she held it up to the shape of the hips and limbs of the wearer.

Judith began writing Sean a letter. It went through several drafts, many of them blotted with tears and thrown away; these were all far more impassioned, even hysterical than the one she sent:

Dear Sean,

I am afraid that my eyes were bigger than my stomach,

as the saying goes, and you were right, the work on your garden has proved too much for me in the end. I've made a good start, I hope you'll agree, and I hope you'll be able to take it from there to your satisfaction.

I wish you well,

Judith

PS Do keep putting down eggshells to deter slugs and snails, and if it's dry, please remember to water, as drought will kill the new plantings very quickly.

On the phone the evening he had her note, Sean sounded shocked; he did not understand what had happened.

'There hasn't been anybody here,' he said.

When he came round to find her at her house later that evening, he appeared so genuinely baffled, she told him.

'Even if Meriel really did come to see me, I didn't see her,' he said. 'Besides, I didn't invite her, and I know nothing about it. Also, it's quite possible for her to come round and for us to have a drink together, surely?'

She wanted to cry out, from the most boring depths of her hurt, 'But how did she get in?'

'And I promise you,' Sean went on, 'you have nothing to fear from her. She has shown no sign of returning, now, or at any time. Nor has Daisy, nor has Sylvie. And not for want of my trying to persuade them.'

Judith flinched.

'Not now, silly. *Then.*' He paused. 'You have a past, too. You have ... Iain.' He looked out of her window on to the garden, which lay in darkness now. 'There are always others. We're old enough to have lives around us. We've travelled old tracks, gone to earth more than once.' He turned back to her. 'Don't be angry about this.'

The groundwork on Sean's garden was done, and so they moved into a different phase, for there was no obvious pretext for their meetings. She had to own up to herself that she wanted to be with him, that he wasn't casually profiting from her employment. Sometimes, she even talked to him unguardedly: unaccustomed new feelings sprang at her, like the flash of a pair of night-seeing eyes from the canal bank when she cycled to and from Sean's, or the brush of her vixen, bushier now from all that peanut butter laid out by Judith (and by neighbours too, no doubt) and flaring for an instant in the long evening light as she swivelled into her earth.

When autumn closed in towards winter, Judith bought some mastic and squeezed out a fillet round the windowpanes of the garden shed to improve the insulation; she found a plant rack and some shelving and installed them, regardless of any possible occupant. There she began potting and layering, bringing on slips and cuttings for the planting she was planning for the spring. She imagined that garden as it would be: her head was moving with pictures from the future, and the past was jostling for attention at the back of the class, sticking up its hands and messing about, calling out 'Miss, gotta go to the toilet'. She was quelling it with her crossest look, but it was disruptive, it wasn't going to cooperate.

In the shed one morning, a woolly hat appeared, a rich rust colour, with a furry trim, tossed into a basket next to a good make of secateurs. Judith did not remember seeing either of them before, any more than Sylvie's skirt (it was Sylvie's, Sean confirmed). She plucked the hat out of the basket and pulled it on, then checked herself in the pane, which against the dark glossy foliage of the new camellia she'd planted beside the shed, acted as a mirror. It suited her: she looked as if she was up to something, something not to be anticipated or understood before it occurred. Still wearing the hat, she went back through the house, and up the stairs, and into the glory hole. She pulled the skirt from its new position on a hanger, and still in her gardening T-shirt, jeans and socks, stepped into its soft folds. She went into the bedroom and made a tentative turn in front of the mirror. She liked the effect: there was something raffish about this outfit. It turned her into a kind of stranger to herself, a new visitor in her own life, and the encounter was not unpleasant.

Back in the shed, she went on thumbing in seedlings, then, using the secateurs, cut up into knubby lengths a good section of iris root she'd sliced from a friend's choked clump. As the night drew in, she began to set it carefully into the flower-bed on what would be the sunniest patch of the garden in the spring.

When Sean came back from work later, she found she enjoyed the sex better than the time before or the time before that. Such satisfaction it delivered, to watch Sylvie hovering there, on the landing outside the bedroom door, in her jacket and tights and boots, but without her skirt.

When a nightdress turned up with the Chinese dressing gown again on the back of the bathroom door a few days later, Judith took a shrewd look at the fabric and the workmanship and appreciated the fine blue lawn with cotton lace trim.

She was humming the theme from one of her favourite pieces of Bach while she let her clothes fall on to the bathroom floor and put on the nightie. When she walked down the stairs and saw Daisy sitting reading in a chair by the fire in the sitting room, she started, of course. But this time, Judith hardly quailed; almost without pause, she turned back on her heel and went upstairs, and standing in the bedroom, pushed her fists into her eyes until the snowflakes needling into her burst into flowers of colour and light, and then she turned on the electric blanket in anticipation, waiting for Sean to come back so that they could do what they liked to do and have sex before supper.

LADYBIRD, LADYBIRD

IMOGEN LIKED CHARITY shops, house clearance sales and junk yards: her very first flat was furnished with Sixties formica and tubular steel, but she'd given away the twiggy hat rack with the bobbles, the beige moleskin beanbag, and the moiré pink kitchen cabinet with sliding glass panels, now that every style slave had to have them. But she still loved the clothes, though these days they'd usually already been spotted as vintage and were no longer a bargain. So she was surprised by the dress in the window of her local PDSA – For Pets Who Need Vets. It was a frock, a real frock with a sweetheart neck-line and a full, gathered skirt in a light cotton with a scatter of a pattern in different colours on a lovely flamey crimson background. She went in, almost breathless when she asked – thinking it might not be for sale, or already sold to someone else – if she could try it on.

Even better, it had a soft lawn petticoat in a paler lemony-pink underneath, as she glimpsed when the old woman serving in the shop began pulling it over the head of the dummy.

'We keep some pieces to bring in the collectors' – she spoke confidingly – 'and this one has a certain je ne sais quoi, don't you think?'

Behind the curtain in the back room surrounded by the tat and the knick-knacks that weren't yet priced, Imogen held the dress against her body and looked at herself in a mirror propped up against the wall. The pattern repeated, it sprang around the frock to a lively rhythm, and she could see herself in ballet pumps with a new belt to replace the one that looked worn, especially at the holes where the wearer's waistline had strained a bit. When she put it on, the fabric danced against her thighs, and the narrow bodice fitted miraculously to her own small breasts, and she could see how it once spun and whirled on a dance floor; it made her want to – well, twist and shout. Not that she did much singing or dancing with Greg, now that they'd been together for fifteen years. Besides, they had to stay in and eat healthily and keep regular hours so that they'd never miss the exact right moment when her hormones were peaking perfectly for that magic outcome, a baby.

They'd been trying. First they hadn't admitted they were trying, but then, when it didn't happen, they started – tests and treatments and thermometers and charts – and now it was like being in training, every moment monitored, controlled, regulated. When a kiss was just a kiss was a world ago and time.

'It's £20 to you,' said the woman serving, when Imogen came out in it. Imogen saw that this old charity volunteer was very thin and silvery all over, with silvery peach fuzz on her face and pale blue eyes when she turned to the light coming from the street outside. She looked like a rare breed of cat and, Imogen realised, must have once been beautiful. 'Our top price and a snip at that. And it has your name on it, love, I can tell.'

When Imogen nodded, she started bundling it up in discarded Xmas wrapping, then stopped. 'What's this? Something in the pocket.' She felt around for the lump inside the fabric, concealed in the folds. 'In an *inside* pocket – ah, a comb! But we shan't grudge you the extra item, shall we? Let's say it's the free gift you get with purchases of £20 or over!' She laughed quaveringly; she almost mewed.

The comb was blue plastic with a tooled gilt clasp; the teeth were bent and none too clean.

'Yes, I'll take that, too,' said Imogen, not knowing why.

She came home light-footed and light-headed; ran a basin of lukewarm water, stirred the soft flakes to a lather, and slowly squished down first the dress and then the petticoat. They gave off a smell of old deodorant and dust. She soaped them tenderly, lifted them out, and added the comb to the now dingy suds. Her mobile began to tweet.

She listened, once she'd hung up the dress to dry. A voice message. Someone was giggling through a snatch of sing-song:

'You look so pretty when you go out
Oh mother mine, oh mother mine.'

It must be someone misdialling – a kid phoning a friend? Funny way to talk, though.

She pressed Reply. It whined unobtainable.

Then the landline rang in the kitchen.

It would be Greg, she thought, saying he was on his way home, his voice full of apology at running late – she was ovulating by her chart, and he knew they had plans. But when she answered, there was a gurgle, as if someone was covering their mouth not to crow with laughter. No word, nothing more.

She'd scrubbed the comb with her nailbrush, and it was drying on a hand towel by the basin. She picked it up, squinted to see if she'd extracted all the old gunge, and seeing it was clean ran it through her hair. Strands lifted off her head, cling-ing to the tines and crackling with sparks. She cried out, and laughing, smoothed down her wild hair.

Her mobile bleeped: a text.

U look sweet in yr nu frock
Come back 2 me, o come back 2 me.

It was signed with a ☺ and two !!

As she was gazing at it dumbly, there was another bleep. Imogen's fingers were so shaky by this time she had trouble pressing the buttons right. This text was a photograph: a blurry, faded, colour snapshot of a baby with a cotton cap on its head.

This time, she switched off her mobile, and turned her at-tention to the dress it could be damp ironed, it might even benefit. She was spreading it on the ironing board when the phone in the kitchen rang:

The flames are close, the fire is hot
Come back to me, oh come back to me
Before they dance around my cot.

She wanted to press 2 and hear the message again, but it had been a real voice this time, and her caller had rung off. She held the receiver to her ear; looked at it; the photograph superimposed itself on the earpiece. She tried 1471: 'The caller withheld the number.'

Running back to the bedroom, she stepped into the dress; it was slightly damp, and leapt and settled around her, aswirl.

She began to feel rushes – fear? Horror? Neither. She wanted to explode, that was it, crow aloud, like that child gurgling, but louder. She was feeling gorgeous; this something was coming from somewhere she didn't understand, but she didn't need to.

When Greg came through the front door, she whispered into her mobile, 'Wait, just wait, this time you will be safe, I promise.'

She turned it off. Then, as an afterthought, she shut off the ring tone on the landline too.

Greg said, edging himself out of the straps of his office backpack, and looking at her with a finger to his temple, 'Let's see, you're Cybill Shepherd in *The Last Picture Show*?'

She shook her head; she suppressed a gale of laughter; she was ablaze, a divinity who could shoot white lightning from quivering fingertips.

'No? Then you're – let's see. Who's the girl, not Divine of course, but the other one, the actress in *Shampoo*?'

'You mean *Hairspray*, silly, and I'm not Debbie Harry.'

They had videos and DVDs and watched them often; it was part of the treatment, to enjoy things together. But Greg often fell asleep, on account of the strenuousness of his new duties.

'This could just about be her, couldn't it?' Imogen pointed down to her frock, then up to her neckline, put her hands on her waist. 'But do you think it's me?'

'It's certainly a frock and a half,' said Greg.

When Imogen wasn't all anxious and business-like and bossy before they had to have sex, it made it easier to – well – do it, and he liked her fizzing and bobbing about like a girl on a night out, sitting on the sofa with the full skirts spread out, shaking out sparks from her hair as she combed it, smiling at him with intent. He started to move towards her. The phone in the kitchen began ringing again. She started; he turned to go to answer it.

'Oh, leave it,' she said. 'I know who it is. It's someone who keeps calling, wants to see me. For some reason.' She tilted herself back on the sofa, plucked at the panels of the skirt to beckon Greg towards her. 'I'm going to keep the frock on. I don't care if you do muss it all up. I want you to. It feels right, somehow.'

It was spring now: nine months to Christmas. Noel, or Noelle – that would be a pretty name for the laughing child who had chosen to come home.

ITEM, ONE TORTOISESHELL BAG

... rectangular, with deep lid, chrome clasp, two curved handles and four internal compartments. Parisian manufacture, *c*.1954

The glowing, mottled panes of my mother's evening bag were puzzling; my pet tortoise was dry and dusty all over, its dark shell grooved and grainy as old timber on a breakwater above the waterline, where the waves never splash to make it gleam in the sun. The pattern on the animal's carapace was squared off, the sections bulging more towards the dome, but neither this mottling nor the shell's lustreless texture looked in the least like the honey-and-toffee translucent dapple of Beata's prize possession.

The animals were cheap at the pet shop in the bazaar; they weren't protected yet. The shell, by contrast, was a luxury material – like ivory, crocodile, or shagreen. But when I say 'my pet tortoise', it's misleading because I had a series of the creatures, each one disappearing in turn. 'It's gone into hibernation,' Beata would reassure me, 'it'll show itself again when the weather warms up.' A tortoise never becomes a pet, not really: petting is limited to tickling it so it'll poke out that troubling ancient head with its dinosaur eye, dull and mineral as a diamond before polishing, or coaxing that low-slung, narrow and lipless mouth to ruminate on leaves. But no tortoise I had ever uttered a sound. Could a tortoise bark? Could it squeal?

The tortoises of my childhood were baffling – perhaps they gave me my closest encounter with the state of bafflement.

Yet, from this gloomy, lumbering creature in its mute pathos, its almost unfathomable antiquity, came the translucent and luxurious material of the brushes that Francis kept on his dressing table and the combs Beata wore in her hair.

The bag was a love gift from early on in her marriage. Francis had bought it for her in a rare moment of largesse from a boutique under the arches of the rue de Rivoli; it was her birthday – her twenty-sixth, I think. If I hadn't been told otherwise, I would have thought it was made like the windowpane sugar on Beata's crème caramel, or a slice through agate – gilded sweetness fused with light set hard through fire or ice long ago. But 'bag' really isn't the mot juste, since it suggests something soft and shapeless, whereas this objet de luxe is rigid and architectural, like a jewel box or some kind of superior picnic kit, but wonderfully delicate: an ornament, a centrepiece, an exhibit to add to the display she'd make every evening she and Francis went out into the Cairene social round.

I prised up the catch on the clasp, the chrome a little peppered by age, and lifted the deep lid on its tiny hinges of copper – one screw has worked loose over the years and the shell has warped a little – and from the empty and silent box rose the hubbub of a warm summer night in Gezira, laughter and snatches of talk, whisperings and exclamations, the clatter of china and chink chink of crystal from the drawing room, blurred names being called out at the door by the suffragi, a car door slamming in the street below, more laughter, the curtain on a verandah slapping in the night breeze from the river below, the shout of a carter with his donkey caught in the melée of the traffic, the patter of casino chips and ricochet of the ball against the rim of a roulette wheel, the spurt of a cigarette lighter being lit, a guffaw from Francis, a car starting up and driving off, at speed, slower traffic from the street moving haphazardly towards the Qasr el-Nil Bridge, the evening call to prayer from the mosque across on the other side, distant music from the barges moored downstream on the left bank of the pulsing river, stars falling into the dark water, Beata coaxing and Beata cooing, Beata waving, flutter flutter, swish swish, with her Japanese-style fan, smoothing the folds of her dress, the rustling cream organza over layered petticoats of tulle, scattered with sequins she'd stitched in arabesques that curled up the bodice and picked up the glitter from her eyes. She had her admirers – she called them cavalieri serventi – and all the time I was still living at home there was always someone in her life who came and went, and Francis sometimes loved him too, but not always.

After Beata died, I heard from Selma, who was her confidante from those days and afterwards, in London, that at one time my mother had come very close to leaving Francis, but that she had stayed with him for my sake, for my sake and my sister's.

'Who was he, Selma?' I asked. 'Please think back.'

'He was quite a high-up, and seemed a bon parti. He was doing some business in Africa. He was mad about her. Everybody was mad about her. But this time it was a near thing, I'm telling you. Thanks be to goodness your mother thought twice about it. He went to the bad. I heard that later he was put in gaol.'

'You must remember his name! What did he do? Who was he?'

'It's all too long ago.' Selma shook her head and gave me the names of some old friends to ask. 'If they're still alive,' she added.

A few months ago, before I'd sorted all her possessions and before I felt able to give away her clothes, a flyer came through the door saying that the *Antiques Market* telly programme was to come to our area, and would be setting up shop in the local library, and we could bring along any mystery objects for the experts to identify and value.

Tortoiseshell is now an illegal substance, its export prohibited under severe penalties, as notices at airports constantly warn travellers. At Gatwick and Heathrow there are those dilapidated Wunderkammern, with their dusty and higgledy-piggledy displays of conch shells and crocodile skins, pelts of rare cats and snakes, ivory tusks and carvings – they also include, often enough, turtle shells and a few gnarled objects made out of them. I wondered what Beata's evening bag would be worth these days, or if it would even be seized.

The programme's young researcher thought the bag was sufficiently unusual to be featured, and I was taken to meet the expert who'd conduct the interview on camera later. She was a young woman called Dido, very long and slender with her red hair in a colourful bandana tied up with a flourish; she had a funny deep voice that made everything she said sound italicised and bristling with exclamation marks.

'Ooh! Vintage contraband!' She picked up Beata's bag, and ran her long hands with their slender fingers tipped in green lacquer over the smooth surfaces. 'Gorgeous! Glamorous! Almost edible, no?' Her fingertips were remembering, through the unexpected temperature, neither cold as metal nor warm as amber, this material's reptilian origin. 'Delicious – but only as a dragon or a python might be. A strong taste. A very strong taste. A fashion accessory for a woman of style, a sensational woman … your mother? Wow, this was your mother's?

'Well, I can see her now in you, yes, that's it.

'A museum – and that's really the best place for such a piece – a real talking point. To explore bespoke artisan industries in Paris couture. On eBay, you'll probably get £200, £300 if you're in luck.

'But I'd keep it if I were you. Take it out now and then. Like a musical instrument, such an item needs a bit of TLC.

'Meanwhile, for the rest of us, faux tortoiseshell, Bakelite best of all, passes all right these days – like faux ocelot, faux zebra. You take your pick, and no harm done!'

She asked me about Beata and Francis and I spoke a bit about them, the life they led in Cairo where my mother would wear her special evening bag from Paris to the tea dances and cocktails and soirées and charity galas and other dos they went to every evening. I brought out a photograph of a Christmas staff party with Beata in the foreground wearing a paper coolie hat with a streamer and smiling in unselfconscious gaiety at the camera, which must have been held by Francis, as he isn't in the picture.

About a month later, a handwritten letter arrived, forwarded from the television company.

The writer had seen the programme and wanted to tell me:

I recognised the bag – it all came back to me, the parties, the fun, that time I was passing through Cairo on my way back from Addis where I was teaching English literature at a school there. It must have been 1954, and your mother – and your father – were wonderfully kind to me.

You reminded me of her – may I ask, is she still alive? She was a marvellous free spirit.

Yours, with best wishes,
Ronnie Quigley

The writing paper was quality rag, the address – in Jane Austen's village of Chawton – nicely set out and embossed, the hand shaky but shapely.

On an impulse, I did not write back a routine acknowledgement as I would normally (if I got round to answering at all), but rang the number included in the address on the headed paper. A quiet, agreeable voice; old but not entirely moribund. We talked a little; the dates fitted, it seemed to me, and from what he said on the phone he'd led an adventurous life, mostly in Africa. He invited me to lunch at a small place he knew in St James's; he would come up to London from where he lived in the country to meet me again, he said, as he had known me when I was a little girl.

I arrived first, on purpose as I wanted to see this old admirer of my mother's, Ronnie Quigley, come through the door, and, if possible, take stock of him before he saw me. It was almost certain he'd be the only guest of his age arriving at the restaurant. But what did I want, now? What did I expect? Did I want him, this one, to be the one for whom Beata nearly ran away from Francis, but didn't because of me and my sister?

This old man, now giving our order to the waitress – two Kirs to celebrate, trout paté for me, soup for him, then Dover sole for two with a bright Pinot Grigio? ('Yes, perfect,' I murmured) – is tall, bulky, with ruddy colour on his veined cheeks and hands; hooded, colourless eyes; leathery jowls; careful good clothes, the collar and tie knotted high to conceal the tortoise neck; but swollen feet in orthopaedic sandals. A widower, he informs me; he clearly has savoir faire and old-world gallantry, he is suggesting the opera, talking of his neighbours in Hampshire, and the gardens that open to the public in his village; this old man in his old school tie is in his mid-eighties, florid and dilapidated, but still, doing well for his age, not altogether implausible in the role of a romantic adulterer in the tropics many decades ago; his old flat clumsy feet mourn the dancing partner who took Beata by storm. Clark Gable, Cary Grant, they were her idea of a man: a certain caddish allure, the effrontery of their self-delight. But then Leslie Howard and, later, Anthony Perkins moved her to tears: the 'gentle' in 'gentleman' matters, she would say. Ronnie Quigley here at the restaurant, drinking his soup with as little mess as possible, could never have been as suave as Clark Gable or as sweetly cissy as Tony Perkins, but you never can tell.

'Could you bear to hear the story of my ... friendship ... with your mother?'

'Yes,' I said. 'I'm grown-up. She's dead. She died five years ago.'

'On a scale of one to ten, how much of the truth can you take?'

'I'm not sure,' I said. I was startled. 'It rather depends what it is. But I would like to know.'

I'd expected the reminiscing to be nostalgic, tender, but I straightened up as Ronnie Quigley was holding a tight smile on his dry, narrow mouth.

There were many things he began saying that matched what I know about those days:

'We first met at a terrific bash your father gave. At the Sporting Club, at Gezira. I was teaching, but I was considering the business I then took up – educational publishing for Africa. So I'd met Francis, of course. We'd common interests, and he invited me along. He was very hospitable. I was immediately overcome by your mother – everybody was. She was – well, you know. Who would have ever imagined a man like your father would be married to such a stunner!'

I shook my head, drank my Kir.

'She sent a note round after that first evening, asking me to come to tea. So it began. She was a free spirit. Your father was so much older, you know that. She was frustrated, stifled – she needed someone younger. I was younger. And more virile. I was that, too. I had the impression they had not been ... well ... lovers for some time when we met.'

I winced, I nodded, I chewed on a piece of bread and paté.

'She was very direct. No, feisty. She was feisty.' He brought out a clipping from a newspaper. 'Look, here's a piece in *The Times* I cut out which talks about the meaning of the word "feisty".

'Your mother all over.'

Over the next few years, work brought him back to Cairo at intervals, he said, from Botswana and Kenya and the Sudan where he was supplying schools and the universities that were just beginning throughout the continent. He'd visit Beata in the afternoons.

'One time, she sent me a note saying she was taking the boat from Alex and to meet her there to see her off. You were there, you were a little girl then. She told you to go and play on the deck where there were quoits and other games, and then she and I ...'

I was following, making pictures in my mind as he was speaking, and they kept assembling and disassembling, between what I remembered of Beata, what I never knew, what I might never have known about her except for this old man with his lightless eyes, who was drinking and eating with appetite as he talked.

'There in the cabin, you know, I showed her ten inches of hard young male, which was much to her liking, and we did it there, in the cabin.'

'No more!' I waved my hand at the old, bluish, dry lips, the rheumy, slightly bulging eyes. 'Please.'

It made no sense; I couldn't bear it to make sense.

There were some corroborating circumstances:

'Your father helped me out, one time. Good chap.' Later, over the Dover sole, Ronnie Quigley went on, 'I'd run into a spot of bother in Addis with the authorities. The Consul there got in touch with our man in Cairo, and he fixed things, but there was some money involved. Francis stumped up, you know. He said he knew Beata liked me.'

But there were also discrepancies: the timings, the places. For one thing, Beata suffered horribly from seasickness: she never travelled anywhere by boat.

And there were other sides to the story Ronnie Quigley told me that veered wildly from what I knew; some won't bear repeating. For she was never bold, my mother, never direct, hungry, never ever 'feisty'. Weepy, guilty, whispering her prayers every Sunday, fastidious and full of decorum, however flirtatious.

I told Ronnie Quigley he had things all wrong, but he said he had told me everything, just as he remembered it.

That was a few months ago and now that I have had time to gather my wits together – and rinse my mind of the confusion and distaste he caused me – I can look at what he told me in a number of ways:

I can give him the benefit of the doubt, and imagine he has simply mixed my mother up with another woman, or with other women who he's been entangled with in the course of what has been, according to his own boasting, a very long and adventurous life.

Or, his mind is going: like a demented and senile ape he's trying to stir up his dead embers by talking dirty to strangers.

Or, he's made it all up: he's discovered a clever way of dating women who catch his eye on television – especially ones who might have a background with nice things. After he told me his so-called memories of my mother and I rebuffed him, he simply returned home and waited for another possible candidate to appear, to whom he could write a charming and mysterious letter suggesting he had known her mother rather well. He could take up Facebook, Facebook dating for Bluebeard, online lonely hearts for senior citizens.

Or I can believe him. I've heard from friends how retrieving the past can lead to disillusion. One young woman I know went looking for the mother who had given her up for adoption – but the first thrill of the reunion soon faded and perplexity set in, with the added sadness of entering a deeper level of estrangement based now on choice, not fate. Recognition in real life feels very different from that enthralled bliss that sweeps over dramatis personae and audience alike when the curtain falls on the foundling refound, the lost mother regained. My mother didn't give me up – she held on, against her own interests perhaps. But meeting her in Ronnie Quigley's story brought me face to face with someone I don't know. The family romance itself sours – the other family whose true child I am or might be brings nothing but disappointment in the end. And besides, when it comes to a stepfather manqué, another father who never was, the romance quest leads astray. My attempt to understand Beata's unhappiness will never be complete. It is possible that it's inspired not by what happened to her, whatever it was, but by my need to find she was more fulfilled than it appeared because she so often seemed deprived, constrained in her marriage to my father, and consequently envious of the freedom that life had lavished on me and my generation.

Or I could be looking for Ronnie Quigley, I could be inventing Ronnie Quigley, because he'd give me a reason not to feel guilty about that unhappiness of hers, that gaiety of hers that had so little chance for expression, guilty that sexual liberation came easily for me in my time and not for her in hers. Even though it would still be my fault that in the end she didn't run away.

LETTER TO THE
UNKNOWN SOLDIER

41 Stannington View Road
West Bar
Sheffield

Dear Jobie,

Since my last letter I have had no answer from you.
We all hope you are safe but it is hard to keep our spirits up. The house rings empty for Mother, she says she
misses your banging the door shut when you come home
and is sorry she bawled at you when you did so. I see
her on my day off from the family, but she feels your not
being there more. I gave you our news in my last but I'm
giving it again in case that last was lost. Miss Edith says
she will keep me on colouring and painting her fancies,
as I am so clever at it, so I shan't have to go to make
shells in the mill with the others next year when I turn
fourteen. I told her the noise and tumult and the thought
of what they're for make dark thoughts come too pow-
erfully. I have added my favourite fancies here so you
can see what your little sister can do – rosemary, that's
for remembrance, says Miss Edith, and pansies, that's

for thought. She draws them on hankies she gets from Tucker's by the dozen and note cards from Apsley's, too, like this paper, and some of them are to be Valentines. They're to have different pictures and borders and she says she'll teach us lettering too and curlicues like this:

Let me be thy Love

Don't laugh – do you like it?

Her older brother Charles – you may hear of him soon she says – he is going great guns in London. He is an artist and has won a scholarship to go on to study in London. She says his works are much appreciated and that he is going to make statues of our boys like you who are giving everything for us and we can be very proud of you. She says maybe he will make your picture! I can see you already in in my mind's eye standing there so grand in your cape and boots and helmet.

But it is hard not to know about you. I pray you are safe.

Miss Edith has helped me with the spelling and other things and she sends you her best wishes for a safe return home.

Please write and send me and Mother your news,

Your loving sister,
May

FORGET MY FATE

I

When Barbara May left her house to walk in the opposite direction towards the corner shop, her steps were drawn to the knot of tension tightening in the street; someone was standing in the middle of the road and the noise of the stalled traffic was mounting. At first, she thought it was a prank. But then she saw that the commotion was being caused by Nino, Nino Sanvitale, her neighbour and a kind of friend from her school, where he'd taught music until he'd retired a few years before.

She stood on the pavement, watching, at a loss what to do as Nino conducted the traffic, airily tickling one driver with an index finger to brighten his rhythm, then patting another to slow her to an andante. Barbara began waving to him, trying to bring him over out of the melée, but he was alight with excitement as he turned this way and that, now sweeping his arm over the cars on the downhill run, now chivvying the other stream that was grinding up the incline.

That stretch of the rise to Highgate is a bad boy's dare to cross, a death sentence for the elderly: a bus route and a thoroughfare for heavy freight, with residents' cars parked on both sides, and she saw that Nino was beginning to lurch and twist as drivers started to hoot at him, leaning out of their windows and shouting. He paid no heed to them and did not seem to notice Barbara either as she tried to get his attention but dared not step out through the angry traffic jam. Flecks of sweat and spittle flew around him; his gestures were choppy and loose, windmilling with clownish heaviness. But he plunged on, his eyes half-closed, his sparse hair, a tangerine glow, awry.

The drivers could have responded with a foot on the accelerator, wipers sawing, tootles and blasts, dips and swells of their radios as if playing a piece by Steve Reich. But she realised that the trouble, which had begun to show at school towards the end of Nino's time there, the garbled words, erratic time-keeping, and sudden blanks, now had him in its grip, and the mood in the road was turning ugly.

She was staff at a former Direct Grant school that had become an Independent, but Nino had been a supply teacher only; he'd come in now and then to give music lessons – piano, chiefly, but he'd also stand in as choirmaster and conductor. At work he'd been a bit of a know-all, but a 'good citizen', as the phrase went, who'd take on any task he could manage – and show grace in doing so. At rehearsals of the school orchestra, Nino would treat the tone-deaf player on the triangle with as much courtesy as the first violins. But because he didn't have papers or formal qualifications, the school had never given him a secure position. All had been lost, he said, in the many upheavals in his life.

When the cars eventually halted long enough for Barbara to make her way to him and fetch him to the safety of the pavement, he didn't know who she was. He was stained, and she smelled the staleness off him; he'd painted in his eyebrows crookedly. His shirt stuck to his chest in dark patches; the tangerine showed white at the roots against his henna'ed, flaking scalp. Nino, the immaculately manicured musician, who wore a signet ring of carnelian engraved with his name in Arabic script and brushed his suits carefully (they'd been made by a tailor in Alexandria – his name was inked on the inside of the breast pocket he had once turned out for Barbara to read), was dandified in an old-fashioned way, and she knew he would be ashamed if he knew the state he was in.

She coaxed him back to the house where he occupied the top flat, which, he always sighed, was sad for his cat, sitting in the upstairs window gazing at birds in flight or in the trees. In earlier days the two of them had often talked together there during break, once they'd discovered in the staff room that they were such close neighbours. Both her children were grown and Desmond, her husband, didn't miss her unless she was very late back. So she'd dawdle behind with Nino, drinking Turkish coffee like toffee in thimbles while he played her old LPs until she began to think crackle was part of the music, like the flaws enhancing a master's ceramics. She heard how he'd grown up among the long-rooted Italian-Jewish community in Egypt after his parents emigrated with his sister and himself, then a tiny baby, from Ancona in 1935 to avoid the Fascists. 'They could sense it coming,' he said, 'like dogs howling long before the earthquake gives its first rumble.' And he jerked his head back and howled, but in a throaty hiss; then brought his face close to hers and grimaced. That was when Barbara first glimpsed the disorder that was already breaking up his mind.

The family settled among other Italians in Cleopatra, a suburb of Alexandria. 'But it wasn't anything like the name suggests – it was a poor suburb. It was a "sink estate".' Nino laughed. 'The women left to become nannies for the families of the rich in Cairo. Nannies, and sometimes, Pappa's ... well, you know what – his *trick*.'

Nino's English was pretty fluent, but he picked up the odd incongruous word or turn of phrase from his pupils. Nino looked Italian and moved his body like an Italian, as if his feet and hands were small and light, though in fact he had pianist's hands with strongly developed muscular pads to the thumb and on the palm. He'd first come to England in the wake of Suez. 'Foreigners' businesses were gradually closed down, one by one, and my father had a small draper's shop near the centre of Alexandria – but all assets were being frozen, property seized, no matter how small. We weren't posh – no way. But it made no difference.'

The evening Barbara found him conducting the traffic, she left him at the door. She made some excuse about not going in. He turned his face to hers, full square, and she quailed from the blind milkiness in his blue eyes threaded with red. But then something clicked and came into shape behind them and he mouthed her name, 'Barbara, Barbara May,' slowly, and then added, 'teaches the girls and boys about Dido and Aeneas ...' His look fell slowly to her lips, and he sang almost soundlessly the thin line of a melody she did not know. Barbara shivered; it reminded her of the time she'd met a parrot, and the bird's black tongue played between the two hooked nebs of its beak and pecked at her coquettishly. Her hand flew to her own mouth to cover it, and she turned and almost broke into a run.

∿

Nino alluded to a wife in the past and mentioned children, but Barbara had assumed they were all long behind him, part of a world of custom and opinion when protestations of hetero-sexuality were necessary to survival.

After Nino died, a note arrived from someone who identi-fied herself without further explanation as his daughter, Bila. Written on a scrap of paper, the note said simply:

Dear Barbara May,
    I found your name on a list my father left, distribut-ing his effects. He specifically wanted you to have the enclosed.
    'Enjoy!
    Yours with good wishes,
    Bila, née Sanvitale

The envelope had arrived by hand. There was no return address. Bila must have been clearing his flat. Had she rung the doorbell? Barbara wouldn't know, and anyhow, she'd prob-ably been at work.

Inside, there was a plain brown folder with a single phrase pencilled on the cover:

Elissa – Cairo, 1950

Holding the folder in her hands, she had a flash: she'd been talking to Nino, grizzling in the staff room about teaching Virgil to sixteen-year-olds, when Nino said, 'Try playing them

Dido and Aeneas, that last lament, with the great, incomparable Flagstad – Kirsten Flagstad. Surely then, Barbara, even the hardest of hard nuts will begin to ...' – his hand passed over his heart – 'to feel. To feel something happening inside. They act tough, but they're not that tough.'

'You don't know the half of it.'

When Barbara first taught Virgil, the class used to snigger and even blush at the cataract of Dido's passion and then her fury. Now the intensity of her love made them snort. They laughed in disbelief that she felt she had to kill herself. Brutally, they wanted her to turn on her lover, kill him instead.

'When she sings "Remember me, but ah! forget my fate", Dido is right, you know,' she'd said. 'She doesn't want anyone to suffer afterwards on her account. She's thinking of us.'

'No, no,' cried Nino, and when he became excited his Italian tones came back more pronouncedly. 'We must forget all that. None of it happened like that – it's all due to that dreadful Roman collaborator! It's all Virgil's invention.'

Barbara was discomfited; he was showing how much he knew, and about her subject. Stiffly, she interrupted him: 'Dido says that because she's ashamed. She's disgraced in the eyes of society and of her world. She isn't really married at all. It's an old story – she's been tricked like a silly goose of a girl. That's what she wants us to forget.'

'But nothing in it is true. Not a word of it. Roman slanders. Official lies. Politics. Piety –'

'Stories and poems don't have to be true!' Barbara was now sure of her ground. 'In fact, they'd be very dull if they followed history – so, good for Virgil, if he did make up such a terrific, tragic love affair!'

'"I think you'll recognise this –",' Nino replied. 'That's what a storyteller always says to capture the audience. And Virgil brings off this great stroke of recognition because his Dido suffers what everyone longs to suffer: extreme passion! It's an ideal state, to love more than one's loved in return. Ah! to be sedotta e abbandonata ... of course it is.' He laughed, quietly, and went on, 'But you can push a story in other directions – ones that are less frenzied. Towards ordinary moments of love and satisfaction and happiness. The big epic poets don't bother with those. They like Dido dead or dying. Widow Dido. Dead as a Dodo Dido. Virgil loves making us watch her throw herself into the flames.'

'That's unfair! We're on her side,' Barbara protested. 'Virgil doesn't admire Aeneas for abandoning her the way he does. He can't help making us feel a kind of ... contempt for his hero, that perfect specimen of the repressed English public schoolboy, compelled by duty, out of touch with his feelings.'

'Virgil had Egypt in mind,' Nino had also said in the course of that conversation, making a sour face as he tasted the cafeteria coffee they were having together in the lunch break at school. 'Dido is an Oriental queen, she is Elissa, the exiled Queen of Tyre, and you know Oriental queens are bad news.'

Before the close of that conversation, Barbara had wanted to get away, but Nino laid his hand on hers: 'One day,' he said, 'we'll talk about Elissa, the true Dido, before Virgil got to her.'

She didn't pull her hand away, though she was uneasily aware of its pressure.

In spite of her irritation, Barbara tried out Nino's idea in her class: she turned on the overhead projector, and an image of

Elizabeth Taylor floated on the screen, her eyebrows in arcs like swallows' wings, her eyes like birds with eyeliner tails; she was supreme in the cobra diadem.

Nino had said, 'There's another story, you know.'

'Look through Dido,' she told her class. 'And what do you see? Cleopatra.'

There were some letters in the folder, still in their envelopes lined with blue tissue paper and addressed in a hesitant hand with curly capitals and lots of loops, the script of someone who does not write very much. The stamps were Egyptian. She held the bundle close to her nose, expecting the perfume of an expensive milieu, jasmine and Turkish cigarettes, but London damp from Nino's cupboard had overlaid them with a mushroomy bloom. Underneath it were some sheets of a text, a carbon copy of something composed on an old typewriter, and several closely written pages of a score.

The first letter was signed in clear letters Banou Zafarin; it was dated 25 March 1949, and was written in French. King Farouk was going to turn thirty the following year, and she was answering the cher maitre's interesting offer to compose a piece to celebrate the birthday. She was polite but eager; she expressed nostalgia for the days when *Aida* was created for the opening of the Suez Canal, when the Khedivial Opera House greeted the haut ton who flowed to Cairo as the guests of Mohammed Ali, no expenses spared. Mme Zafarin was recently widowed, it turned out, and her husband's brother, who was now her guardian, had a position of some influence at court – hence the indirect approach Nino was attempting.

As the correspondence grew, she talked more often of her

two daughters, Amina and Zubayda, whom Nino was teaching, and of her husband, who had been very musical, and how she herself loved to play. She began to confide: Abdel, her beau-frère, did not share the qualities of her own beloved husband.

On the face of it, the correspondence stayed formal and reticent. Each letter from Mme Zafarin began, without variation, 'Cher maître' and never progressed to 'Nino' or even 'M. Sanvitale'; but the phrase began to acquire a skittish, ironic tone, as if it were becoming a pet name between them. Yet, beneath the courtly phrasing and necessary decorum, Barbara could sense excitement rising: the rhythm of their sending (the first twelve letters arriving in as many days) conveyed how Banou Zafarin was glimpsing the chance of something igniting. Her writing became more rapid and fluid as her hopes grew that Nino's plan would lift the stultifying round of ladies' lunches and wealthy widows' charity dos.

In her tentative hand, Mme Banou Zafarin informed the cher maitre, Nino, that his idea had been received with interest at the Palace and the beau-frère would soon be raising it with their splendid young ruler.

Barbara had agreed with Nino that they would have another Dido-Cleopatra conversation, another time. But that time had never come. Rumours about his forgetfulness grew, his air of worn-out cosmopolitanism became a reproach, as if he were posted at the school gates, begging. There were stains on his forlorn tie. An inspector recommended restructuring, and Nino's arrangement, such as it was, wasn't renewed.

II

Barbara smoothed the onionskin, brittle with age. She began to read:

ELISSA, OR THE TRIUMPH OF AFRICA

Lyric drama in six tableaux
DRAMATIS PERSONAE

Elissa, queen of Tyre ...... *Mlle Amina Zafarin (soprano)*

Sychaeus, her husband, ... *to follow (mezzo-soprano)*
a priest

Pygmalion, her brother .... *Mlle. Zubayda Zafarin*
(mezzo-soprano)

Iarbas, king of Mauritania, ... *to follow (mezzo-soprano)*
suitor for Elissa's hand *to follow (mezzo-soprano)*

Assassins; Tyrians; .... *Chorus of the schools*
Mauritanians; Carthaginians; *of Cairo and Alexandria*
virgins and nymphs; courtiers
and attendants etc etc

The story so far:

In Tyre, principal city of the ocean-going Phoenicians, one of the richest kingdoms in the ancient world, and originator of the alphabet, the king is dying. Elissa is his heir, but her brother Pygmalion is enraged and plots to take the throne.

(Aria, here, for a mezzo, and your younger daughter, Madame, has a very pleasing, rather deeper timbre than her sister.)

'The historical Elissa is NOT a woman who gives up in despair or shame. She is a strategist, the founder of a nation, a North African nation. *Bref,* a new woman.

Barbara turned the pages of the score, following the scenes: the murder of Sychaeus in the temple of Hercules as he was making a sacrifice to the gods, by assassins hired by Elissa's own brother.

It was a hugely ambitious, sprawling work, Barbara could see, filled with passionate laments (*'Darkest of destinies'*, C minor) and, after Elissa has escaped and set sail for Carthage, a rousing chorale (*'Africa! Africa! The future of our people!'*)

The passage was marked in the margin:

– C'est très bien! J'aime beaucoup!

At one juncture, when Elissa, en route to her new city, cheerfully takes on a shipload of sailors' sweethearts to populate Carthage, Mme Zafarin became quite bothered:

'Come, come, cher maître, you must be joking!'

She proposed instead that the young girls play peris and nymphs:

'This would be much more appropriate for jeunes filles bien élevées, and besides the costumes will be much more attractive.'

The whole gigantic work came to a grand finale with the marriage of Elissa to the king of Mauritania, and a wedding march (allegro vivace, D major).

III

So: no Aeneas, and a *school* production, with the principal roles given to the daughters of Mme Zafarin, Nino's correspondent.

Barbara explained to her husband, when he came in that evening, that unaccountably she, who couldn't play the piano or sing a note, had been left a score by a colleague who had died that year. She added that he was 'That Egyptian – with the carrotty dyed hair – you remember him, don't you?'

Desmond looked vague, but when Barbara frowned, he said, 'Ah, yes, indeed I do. Left you something, did he? How very nice.'

'Can't think why,' said Barbara, fighting impatience. Nino's bare-faced flattery of the fat Egyptian monarch was pretty sickening, she thought, but even so, had there ever been a smidgeon of a chance that Nino could have brought off this vast work he was planning?

'Cher maitre', wrote Mme Zafarin. 'Thank you for the score, which I have received safely. I have begun to play. The music is agreeable but ...' She needed a fellow player, she wrote, as Nino had composed the piano medley for four hands and so far, even under his tuition, her daughters were not quite up to it.

Barbara looked again at the music in the folder – and there it was, another pair of hands was involved. The piece was a duet for four hands, with Nino the teacher taking the harder part, the student at his side on his right the less demanding music.

She thought back to the times Nino had invited her in, charmed her at his table with his records, his conversation, his wine, his coffee. Had she missed something? But then she paused – she was a woman who did not like to imagine things.

'The idea of taking a picnic in the desert during the interval before the last act begins is very tempting,' wrote Mme Zafarin. 'We should see whether His Royal Highness's birthday coincides with the full moon. However I do not think, *Monsieur*, that you should place so much emphasis on what you term "the glorious history of feminine influence and female power in this northern part of Africa". After all, we shall be celebrating the King's birthday, not his sisters'!'

Then Barbara found another letter, the last in the series:

'Cher maitre, Je regrette …'

Banou Zafarin was leaving Cairo for the summer to spend it far from the whirl of the city. It was too hot to stay in town, she said. 'If you yourself happen to be in Alexandria this summer,' she went on, 'you will be able to find me with the children on the beach at Sidi Basr 2.

'PS I am having our piano brought from Cairo so that my girls will be able to keep up their practice.'

Did Mme Zafarin mean something particular when she wrote that it was beginning to get too hot in town? Did Nino find a way of joining her for the summer in Alexandria? Of continuing the piano lessons?

It seemed that that was where their contact on the page came to a close. And when something else began?

Barbara could not help wondering, even though she was not given to fantasy, why Nino had wanted her to glimpse this moment in his past, as she felt the sharp prick of intimacies unattained.

IV

When Barbara and Nino used to talk, in the staff room at the school or in his flat after teaching, she'd always felt the need to get away from him: work, home, her own routine, friends and family called to her in a kind of obbligato pulsing away under whatever tune Nino was playing. She realised that even though she liked being with him, he'd never mattered – or rather she had never noticed that he mattered. His attention flattered her but didn't reach her at any depths at all. Which is why she could leave him at the door after she found him in the street that last time she saw him.

Then she began to remember more things about him, how he liked to say, 'Think of the world, think of your world, like a band. Everyone in the band is different. Everyone has a different voice. But together you can express something effectively. You can charm us – as well as yourselves – hold us captive to what you are playing. Make that moment mean something that is not like the rest of life, that is for a time the opposite of dull.'

She began to see something in herself that was uncomfortable to admit, uncomfortable in a different way from her moments of uneasy contact with him when he was alive. Nino had presented her with a design that didn't possess familiar features; the plot he was living in wasn't one she recognised. He had said to her, 'I think you'll recognise this,' and she'd taken him for one thing; or rather, she'd mistaken him.

It would all be so much easier, she thought, if you could direct your own life's affections the way you can make up a story and move the characters in it, change their ways of behaving and modify their feelings, stretching them according to your highest expectations of yourself. But something inside you stays stubbornly fixed, and unlike a story, won't let itself be prodded and shaped.

But then not all stories are supple.

Perhaps the usual story of Dido, Virgil's great tragic queen, is recognisably close to everyone's experience: she was remembering how Nino remarked, It's the fate of us all to love more than we are loved in return. Recognising a particular story does add to its pleasure: it's safe too, it's home. Funny that tragic self-killing should be such a place of satisfaction, of comfort. Maybe there is an alternative story – one that isn't so compelling, but one that fits closely, if not obviously, to another kind of experience, a little more commonplace, with a happy ending. That story also invites us to enter but it is harder to notice. The voice is fainter when it says, 'I think you'll recognise this.'

Hesitantly, Barbara showed the score of the duet to the school Music Director; when he tried it out on the piano (she had to nudge him), he was intrigued – much to his surprise. He began mentioning it to friends. One of these, a trombonist who lived with someone involved with arts funding, showed it in turn to the director of the Kempley Music Festival. The programme he was planning for the summer included a strand, 'Cross-currents: East Meets West', and it was to feature works by composers from countries along the shores of the Mediterranean, Arab, Israeli, et al, including some of the earliest electronic music written by a compatriot of Nino's, Halim el-Dabh (who had won first prize in the Piano competition at the Cairo Opera House in 1942). So the director copied the score to the celebrated P— sisters, star performers of the 2008 season, and Yvette and Tanya P— were captivated: besides, they had Algerian roots, for one set of grandparents had been born in Oran.

The *Suite Levantine* was full of poignancy and sweetness, of life and laughter, of fun and mischief, they said; it was flirtatious; it had some of Busoni's architecture and melancholy, of Poulenc's ironic wit and Satie's playful spirit. But it also had its own chromatic harmonies and its own pulse, in which they could detect something definitely non-European.

Six Egyptian Songs, or Suite Levantine by Nino Sanvitale received its première at the Kempley Music Festival on June 25 2008.

Barbara was invited to contribute a note to the Festival programme. She found it difficult, and struck out one line after another. When the deadline arrived, she sent what still seemed to her awkward, vapid clichés. But she couldn't find another way.

'Nino Sanvitale was an unforgettable character,' she began, 'with what used to be known as a mysterious past, some of which infuses the musical compositions that he was too modest to talk about and bring to our attention when he was alive. The *Six Songs* were first discovered among his papers after his death, half a century since they were first written but as fresh as if conceived yesterday.' She went on to give some background for the story of Elissa, 'the other Dido', and the opera that never was.

DOLOROSA

'I DO HAVE A core, Lucy, I know it. I'm still looking for mine, but I know it's there.'

Our friend and host Laurent was repeating what he'd been saying, to get a rise out of Lucy now that she was back from her post. He exhaled the words again in a dreamy languor, watching the smoke curl up from the water pipe on the mother-of-pearl inlaid tabouret: 'Inside and outside are as arbitrary as the constellations in the night sky ... each of us is edgeless.'

'I'm not convinced,' said Lucy, taking the bait and flinging herself down on the sofa beside him, and spilling a pile of books from her rucksack. 'Retro Satanas! I say to you, my friend. In spite of my deep and total respect for you, for your mind and – your hospitality, I believe there is something else besides this.' She reached out and pinched Laurent's arm.

'Ouch!' he said, and sleepily breathed in more of the fragrant smoke.

Lucy had tried being a nun, then a sannyasin, now she was working for one of the aid agencies here in the war zone; she was weird, that was the consensus in our group. For myself, I was intrigued, though I shared the general embarrassment.

'She has a core – it's her heart,' one of us put in, a little mockingly – we found her mawkish in her overt compassion (most of us were cultivating hard-boiled cynicism, to ward off the horror).

'No, it's in her DNA,' said the young man from Hull, in a serious tone.

'Or in her liver,' sang out another of our ad hoc band in a Nina Simone voice.

'She means the soul,' someone muttered. 'You know, once a Catholic ...'

It was the autumn of 2006 in Damascus, and we were there to help. Though help wasn't what anyone could do at all adequately. We were all volunteers – students, activists, teenagers, grannies – from all over the place. While the shells roared and whined around us, we talked, we smoked, we brought in food, we talked some more. We were each of us flying from the world we knew into a new one – mocking one out of existence, struggling to dream another into life.

'Let it go, Lucy,' I exclaimed. 'Don't get stuck in that sad old humanistic religious bounded self. Join us as we flow into one another! We're communicating vases. No boundaries. No antipathies. Oceanic in our being – infinitely malleable and with infinite capacity for elective affinities!' I was breathing in the sweet heavy shisha with Laurent. 'The new person isn't a single atom in the vast universe but is each and every one a universe!'

'Why yes and no,' said Lucy, shaking her head and closing her eyes.

She'd been at the children's holding centre at the hospital where the ones who've become separated from their families are kept until ... until they're found. Or so it's hoped. After a certain time, if nobody comes to claim them, they'll be moved to a different place, a more permanent institution. An orphanage. Like some of us, Lucy's been working with the team painting the walls of the room that's going to be used to make music and paintings with the children. In times of war they forget such things and when you forget to play, life begins to lose the struggle with death. But with music and dancing you can keep the tiny light lit inside them and breathe on it. At least that's the hope we were holding on to.

Lucy was saying, 'Food, warmth, someone to hug you … but a child needs something else as well … We all need somebody to … keep each and every one of us in mind.'

'Oh don't bring in God, for fuck's sake. He's either a complete fuck-up or he's forgotten about us.' This was the rationalist from Hull, again.

'I don't mean God, I mean that I don't exist to myself unless someone else holds me in mind.' She paused. 'You're not objecting to that much?'

There were stirrings, but no protest aloud.

After taking a long breath on the pipe, Lucy went on, 'You'll think I'm cracked, and maybe I am. It's a mad world, my masters. But I've had a vision …'

The atmosphere in our digs tensed, palpably. One or two of us caught each other's eye.

'I was at the hospital very early this morning – or very late last night, whichever way you want to look at it – and we had to evacuate to the basement, as usual.'

There were nods at this – others had been on duty too.

'At first there was a lull in the bombing from the ridge, and everything was very quiet except for the small noises of movements children make in their dreams when they're missing things – their mouths eat the air, their eyes search, under closed lids, for a face they know. Then the whirr of a missile began homing towards a target: it seemed close, very close, and it was drawing closer. I ran to the window. A nurse and a doctor came and joined me. We wondered about waking the children, taking them down to the basement. We watched the first missile hit – somewhere to the north of us, in the business district, we thought.'

'Actually, they hit wide and destroyed a street where absolutely nothing happens except people's homes,' someone else said, under her breath.

'Then, in the huge mass of dirty smoke filled with rubble and timbers and debris that boiled up from the impact into the first light of day, I saw a figure, swathed in dark clothing, only her face showing, streaked in blood and grime and sweat and tears. It was a woman with her mouth howling, a black hole. I pointed to her, asked my companions watching with me if they could see her too – but they said no. "Look, there," I said. "Why, yes, perhaps," one of them replied. Then the other said, "It's all in your imagination." And seemed annoyed.

'I turned back to walk through the children's ward, and the second missile hit closer. Then the turmoil began – you know – the staff began waking the ones who could walk and bundling the ones who couldn't into wheelchairs.

'I was trying to be of some use. Then I saw her again, this time in the ward, that veiled figure of smoke and ash and blood and tears, stooping over the face of every child and scanning it closely as we were waking them and began hurrying them down to the basement. I tried to talk to her, ask her what she wanted. She didn't seem to hear me as she moved on, from one child to another – you couldn't stop her search. She reached one little girl, who in her weariness and hurt was struggling against being moved, and the woman gave a sudden piercing cry and, pulling back the covers to scoop up the little girl lying there into her arms, whispered her name, "Zeinab, Zeinab, it's you."

'*You*, you see – the only one, you and none other, the uniquely precious one. The daughter she was searching for, who she's been holding in mind.

'And as she said her name over and over, I saw them rising up together, she holding her Zeinab by the hand, and the little girl floating wide as if weightless like a cosmonaut. They were transfigured as I watched: the filthy woman now a pillar of shining cloud, the listless child rosy and laughing as the up-draught caught her, like gossamer spun into the air.'

There was a silence, fraught with our common discomfort, and Lucy, sensing it, said, 'You all think it's all in my imagination, too, don't you?'

I wanted to do something to ease the rift that had grown between us around the table, so I said to her, quietly, 'It's what you believe – and belief makes all kinds of things happen.'

SEE NO EVIL

'THAT COFFEE MACHINE you ordered from Rome's on the dock now, and the man there's insisting that you must go down in person and be there when they open it, so as to see there's no jiggery-pokery.'

'Who's he? Put him on the line, Georgina, and maybe I'll be able to get it through his thick skull that it's out of the question.'

'The package's addressed to you personally and Customs require that the addressee take delivery. I can't do it for you, Dr Earle.'

'This country's impossible! Fifteen people make a parliament, three judges for the whole damn place, and for a coffee machine you have to have the whole caboodle as if … ?'

'Yes, that is the picture.' Georgina's voice was tart.

'Play-acting cadres. It could be Cuba.'

'In Cuba they don't have cargo coming in from Rome, Italy, Dr Earle. And this is your own native land, and so you can't be saying you're outside of it.'

'Tsk, Georgina. You know they don't listen to me.'

'Huh-uh, Dr Earle. They like to see you in town once in a while. And see what you're going and buying when you're away from home.'

'All right, I'll go down to the harbour office. Let them know I'm on my way, Georgina.'

'I'll find Rob, and he'll drive you into town.'

'There things you've to do in town, Georgina?

'Huh-uh, Dr Earle.'

Dr Diogenes Earle could no longer drive himself: cataracts. Next time he was in Berkeley for his annual teaching visit, he'd have the op. But he kept postponing it. The prognosis was good for this kind of procedure, and yet ...

His eyes were black as lava pebbles on the surf line, with such a gleam on them that one time long ago, when he was going to a party at the High Commissioner's for the Queen's Birthday or some such date, his wife Evangeline had taken his chin and tilted his head towards hers as they stood in the hall waiting to be announced. He had thought she was going to kiss him, but instead she told him to keep still and not blink while she adjusted the angle of her hat in his irises.

The espresso machine of gleaming chrome, with a gilded eagle poised for take-off from its imposing crest, had arrived at the docks less than two months after he ordered it. He was pleased: the banana boats were efficient carriers, their sailing routes, the same ones that had transported his forebears westwards, were still governed by the world's turning and by the *alizès*, the lovely chasing winds, according to their season.

'Rob, you think the coffee machine from Italy will fit in this car?' Georgina asked.

'We could take the truck ...' Rob looked at her for reassurance that his decision was justified.

She took charge: 'Rob'll drive the truck down for the machine as soon as we've seen to all the red tape and fine tuning of the paperwork.'

Then she opened the car door, let herself into the passenger seat, and nodded towards Diogenes to indicate he should sit in the back and demur no more.

As the car descended the slope towards the town and the harbour, Diogenes Earle anticipated with pleasure how he would pass by Peony's later with Georgina and they'd have a drink on the verandah; maybe dinner there too – the house pepper soup, a spiced fricassée of chicken and vegetables, followed by some coconut ice cream – though coconut was one of those lurking devils that leaked into your blood supply and furred it up, goddammit. Who would think that pale scented flesh was poisoned with cholesterol? At Peony's bar, La Rose des Vents, Dr Earle would become Diogenes again, to everyone, including Georgina, and he could bandy the old badinage with Peony, sparring partner, old time lover:

> I'm no nosy parker, but Mamma, tell me why
> Young white meat have such dark hair down there
> While old black Theresina's all snowy white?
> Heigh ho, ho heigh, Mamma, jus' tell me why?

'The trouble with the world today,' Dr Earle, winner of the Braestrup International Prize for Biological Research, was saying to Peony after he finished laughing (though he had heard it before), 'is that jokes like this are finished, over, not to be spoken, not to be heard.'

'Not here, they're not,' said Peony. 'We'll not be gagged, oh no, not me, not you.'

A calypso king came in and sat down with them; name of Sad Sack, old man with a banjo in his hand and six gold chains thick as gift-wrap ribbon hanging against his wrinkled rhino hide chest. He was saying, 'Diogenes, the trouble is ...' he called him Diogenes, as everyone did outside the laboratory precinct, from long before he won the big prize and with it global renown – 'the old languages is dying. Creole, patois, going going, under the influence of TeeVee Miamee: 32 stations beamed at you and me.'

'Yes,' said Dr Earle. 'I came back to get away from that.'

It was true, too. He used his prestige, his success, his name, his life's work in immunology to fund the Institute in the hills of this Leeward Island in the Caribbean, where, beyond the morne, in the middle of banana and coconut groves stretching on all sides, he was working with his team on an enzyme that contained the clue, or so he felt sure, to the metabolisation of HIV into AIDS.

The indigenous vervet monkeys the lab used had been providing for five years now the basic material for the wonder drug that had the capacity, it seemed from widespread trials, to delay onset of the full-blown virus. In the early mornings when he was a child growing up on the island and waiting for the school bus to come bouncing by, the young Diogenes, dressed by his mother in immaculate shirt and shorts of his school uniform, had glimpsed the monkeys springing in the tangle of the breadfruit and mangoes and immortelles that grew in the gullies of the morne. They shrieked and hooted above, a barely visible syncopation in the foliage. A mother, with a young monkey clasped to her breast, would leap from frond to frond, picking the child mangoes in the trees, her lovely, clever tail like an interrogation mark over the folding star of her anus. They were quick and educable, too, test creatures with an aptitude to learn from the experiments he conducted. He loved their small, scholars' faces, with puckered foreheads and twitching brows, and eyes that revolved as if they were considering their miraculous agency in human health with proper wonder. Buddhists are right, thought Diogenes, to venerate monkeys' discretion, and set them up as counsellors, their long narrow subtle fingers clamped to their eyes, their ears, their lips: See no evil. Hear no evil. Speak no evil.

The bodies his research would help keep alive required intervention, allopathic stratagems to forestall the spread of disease, and the quietism of otherworldly metaphysical monkeys could never control the forces of chemical and biological structures gone awry, as he and the team struggled daily to do in the lab. The animals lay in another kind of silence on the operating tables, their wizened hands flopped alongside their paler chests and bellies, their heads thrown back like beach riff-raff after a night on home-distilled rum, as the team worked to extract the necessary cellular tissue.

Earle's thoughts roamed uneasily as he looked over the company around the table in La Rose des Vents: Sad Sack and Peony were still doing the dozens. He caught a fragment, and leaned towards her: 'You, Peony, you have a dirty big mouth ...'

'You's growed so tall, Doctor Diogenes Earle! Soon nobody see your face up there, only that haystack of hair up inside your nose.'

She was roaring with laughter. She knew how to scald him with her tongue; and to do other things with it, too. But the thought of that other wearied him, tonight, for anything that drew attention to his age these days wearied him. The last honorary doctorate had taken him to a big city and another five-star hotel where the suite they'd given him sported a bed big enough for an orgy of six; he'd forgotten his lens cleaning fluid and so had gone out to the local all night drug store, where he'd found the object of his need in aisle 3 under the direction of a contemptuous pharmacist in none-too-clean overalls. But before he reached 'Eye Care' he'd passed under the sign 'Incontinence'. There he took in – without wanting to – stacks of nappies for adults, sized and graded for absorbency, in packs larger than babies' Pampers, with diagrams of their ingenious fastenings and padding for extra comfort and lack of odours.

American TV had accustomed him to slim, sweet-voiced, grey-haired, well-preserved and no doubt pinched and tucked former beauties recounting their constipation and haemorrhoids. But the 'Incontinence' section sent him back to his luxury suite and all its playthings in such sad heart he couldn't even try the Adult channel, and instead curled up between the cool and expensive fabric of the sheets on his enormous bed, feeling that his genitals had shrivelled up to the size of slugs and his bowels would shame him if he ever tried to have a fuck again.

His problem was very clear. Women liked famous men, but access to them became trickier the more visible he became. As honours grew, so did wearisome company, with a tendency to interfere in the successful outcome of an attempt at seduction. If he took Mrs Earle (Evangeline was most cordially included in all these invitations), he escaped the terrors of solitude in those capacious beds and minatory aisles. But Evangeline did not enjoy travelling any more and would not put up any longer with the tedium of official lunches, dinners and those obligatory visits to colleagues' labs and research establishments.

Even if a new lover was ... well, there could be many disappointments in novelty, he knew. Occasionally a woman could not see him at all but only the story she could tell her colleagues afterwards about making out with Dr Diogenes Earle. But even so, the risk, the discovery, the variations, made the attempt exciting in itself. He was an experimental researcher, always had been.

Nobody else heard Peony's taunt that evening, or bothered to take it in, but it smarted, and he stared out across the soft blur of darkness to the town lights between the morne and the sea.

He knew that the Italians, on the occasion of his most recent prize, a medal with many thousands of euros attached, would have turned a blind eye if he'd taken another woman with him. He could have invited Mignonette, his on-and-off young lover, who lived in town where he could sometimes visit her if she was feeling like letting him and he could fit it in between Georgina's protectiveness at the lab and Evangeline at home. But he'd gone alone, and he'd ordered the coffee machine on an impulse one morning after he had been wrapped all night in memories of Mignonette's skin and smell, the close silken weave of her flesh and the peach fullness of her lips, above, between, below, and how she whimpered at the suck and stroke of his tongue and how he felt the tips of her nails on his buttocks where she pulled him deeper into her. In Italy, she might have stopped her objections, which changed daily but couldn't be gainsaid: his position, his wife, his other women, her age, her future. He knew enough about women: Mignonette wanted more from him in return.

Maybe he should offer to divorce Evangeline.

He and Mignonette were flesh of one flesh, he felt, so close when interlocked and laced that he thought the sweetness of it might change his outer as well as his inner self, and that he would look in the mirror afterwards and find himself dipped and renewed like one of the oil drums under the hammers of the steel pan makers, polished to a flashing shine and tuned to a ringing note. He thought that Mignonette even looked like him, perhaps through certain quirks of shared ancestry (a Scots planter in the shadows?) – at a shark sandwich stand on the north shore one day, Mignonette had been taken for his daughter by the vendor, and he'd felt proud.

He remembered leaning over Mignonette, so close he could see into the fibres of her irises; they were smoky-grey with spokes of gold around the dark well of her pupils, dilated in the light of a single bedside lamp; he felt a rush through his heart and limbs, spearing him into a five-limbed sea creature, all consciousness blazing in the pleasure at the crossing of his groin; her white bed, with its thin mattress in the small sparely furnished flat in town, hung in his mind's eye. Maybe he should propose a grand hotel – one of the tourist palaces further up the coast – but you needed to book, it was high season, and besides, he wasn't sure she would agree, without more assurances from him, to spend the night with him in a place where he would be made a fuss of, clamorously.

He would phone her now. He signalled for the bill, and without glancing at it, unfolded some notes and laid them down, waving away the protests of the gathering. A look shadowed Georgina's eyes; she was always vigilant, and it both gratified him and annoyed him. He avoided responding, yawned, said he was tired, he had a breakfast meeting with a journalist from New York; the company guffawed, ribbed him, but he rose, smiling, on the gusts of their chaffing. On his way out, he stopped to kiss Peony and throw in extra for more booze for the company to drink after he was gone.

The next day, he was meeting Larry Turner, the journalist from the *Washington Post* for lunch, not breakfast; he said he wanted to see more of the island, and had hired a car, a sporty red Japanese model. On an impulse Diogenes asked him to pass by Mignonette's to see if she'd come with them, and she was in a sweet mood, as it turned out, and quickly tied some light cotton wrap scattered with tiny stars around her long limbs, and fastened sky-blue sandals on her narrow feet with their silver nails and ankle bracelet. Just the sight of her, bending over to do this and that, smoothing herself and nodding into the small mirror on her bathroom wall, gave Diogenes Earle the sensation that he'd been grasped by a sky goddess and dipped in a fountain of Jouvence. He laughed and patted her on the bottom as she went through the door, and then she tossed her head crossly, but she did not turn back.

They took the road out of town to the east shore where the coast was jagged, the rocks fretted by the Atlantic tide rips and the coconut palms arched like the ribs of Gothic vaulting in colder places. Or, as Diogenes Earle thought privately, like girls throwing their hair about as they thrashed sitting on top of him.

They stopped at a crab-and-beer bar on the beach; took seats at a crooked wooden table with a gingham plastic cloth, secured by drawing pins that had rusted in the salt air. Diogenes let himself enjoy the breeze lifting off the sea; the criss-crossing lines of foam chasing up and down the sand like a flame running rapidly along a fuse laid to a firework. He rarely had the chance for such an outing during the week, especially now he could no longer drive himself, so he made it hard for Turner to embark on the interview; besides, Mignonette was communicative, she had taken him in hand, and was charming the young American visitor, of course. She'd been going to personal-growth therapy; she'd made all kinds of discoveries about herself, it was weird what you could forget or never suspect. It was pleasant to listen to her, almost like standing under the strong jet of a shower after a hot day; when she was animated, her eyes seemed to shoot golden lights, and she had a way of twisting on herself that drew attention to her soft in-between-esses as she sat at the wooden table, occasionally drinking from the melting bottle of beer that had come, frosted, from the icebox whirring to a portable generator under a clump of allamanda at the back behind the shed.

She was saying, how, at the age of fourteen, she'd been doing her science homework:

'Shit, my father volunteered to help and the next thing, there was all this heavy breathing and he was touching me up and putting his hideous hot sweaty hands up my legs ...'

Diogenes Earle put down a crab claw.

'Mignonette,' he said, 'you know I dislike a dirty mouth – I think you could spare us the details of this horror.'

She had twisted differently coloured ribbons in her hair, creating cords that she'd then tied behind on the nape of her neck; Diogenes didn't altogether grasp the architecture of this new style, and it looked forbidding to the caress of a hand; but it made the narrow column of her neck seem even more slender and her eyes even larger: he was reminded of the way a young vervet turns and stares at a stranger, before burrowing back into its mother's fur. At that earliest stage, he reflected, the babies had not yet learned to imitate warning signals, the ak-ak-ak of repeated scatterfire telling of the approach of a stranger.

'That's just awful.' Larry Turner looked flushed, concern emphatically crinkling his eyes.

By contrast, Diogenes realised, he had sounded callous. But why was Mignonette bringing up these things now, and telling this American? Things she had never told him, her lover, things not to be bandied about with strangers, like so much small talk.

He wanted to cry out, We are lovers, for God's sake, we have been the closest two people on this earth can ever be. He wanted to pin her down against the bed and kiss her throat and eyes and mouth and breasts. He wanted to beg her, Don't appeal to this young hotshot from Washington with your stories, don't make monsters of old men like me. You don't know the power you have over us.

A silence fell, and grew lumpy; the breeze brushed through the palm fronds and seemed to swell. The journalist looked out pointedly across the beach to where some young boys were playing with a ball; Diogenes signalled for the waiter.

Larry Turner then put his first question to his subject – as Diogenes knew, it was always at the coffee stage that the real argument was raised. Here, by the beer-and-seafood shack on the beach, there was no coffee, but they ordered another beer

– though Mignonette, the same new vacancy in her face, told him no.

'What are you doing about the growing protests by animals rights campaigners against your kind of research, Dr Earle?'

Diogenes pulled himself back from his daydream, closed down the image of the young Mignonette stuttering alarm cries as one family member after another fondled and molested her sparse baby fur, and concentrated on the journalist.

'Oh, we torture animals, and we smile ...' He bared his teeth. 'We're worse than beasts, we're Mengele and Eichmann and Stalin's death-camp doctors all rolled into one ...' He broke off, pleasantly enough, holding his grin.

Diogenes put his hand on the young man's tape recorder, tapped it and said: 'Turn it on. Is it on now? All right: here is what you are going to hear from me: epilepsy, diabetes, cancer, heart disease, emphysema, asthma – anyone you care about suffer from these conditions? AIDS? If we can find some ways to forestall the fatal consequences of these illnesses – and not only for the sufferers but for all those around them who watch them suffer, and for society and the economy. Let's talk turkey, society and the economy have to support many sick and failing members. We hardly expect to find remedies, we're not into playing God, you do realise, Mr Turner – we are perhaps allowing a child someone loves to grow up as other children do, allowing a parent to survive to bring up his or her offspring, allowing loved ones to continue to live together. Monkeys are our brethren, but they are not our children. And you are welcome to inspect any time to see the operating conditions in which my team works. We could use humans

– that's what the Nazis did. If this animal rights stuff contin-
ues, we may have to recruit volunteers: is that something you
desire?'

Mignonette interposed, brightly, 'Dr Earle had a British
education, you know. He is very ironical.'

Diogenes softened his outburst with another show of
laughing; and called for the waiter.

Then he turned back to the journalist. 'In truth, we make
the animals as comfortable as possible. We're grateful to them
for their collaboration in our endeavours, we respect their
role: without them there would never have been the break-
through we've made with the new T-cell inhibitors. We're not
testing shampoo, you know.'

'This is on me, sir,' said Turner.

'On your paper?'

'Sure.'

'Then you may go ahead and pay,' said Diogenes Earle. He
gave another laugh. 'We're all United States colonials now.
Everyone waiting on their green card.'

'You don't know what it's like, when you haven't got one,'
said Mignonette. She was still staring straight past him.

He could recommend Mignonette for postgraduate work
in the States, of course. Then maybe she would meet him
there, stay with him there. Maybe a drama course? There
were enough affirmative action initiatives for overseas students still in place.

Two boys scrambled up to the verge and hailed the bright
new car the journalist had hired. They were skinny, tall,
dark-brown kids; one held a machete, the other a bunch of

coconuts, which he held up and waved into the car's rear-view mirror.

Diogenes, sitting sideways on the back seat, tapped Larry to stop the car.

They reversed down the road.

'Ever had the milk straight from the nut?' he asked Larry. 'Have some. And for you, Mignonette?'

'I like the jelly,' she said. And then to Larry, 'The soft flesh inside.'

'If you've only had the dried kind, you'll be surprised,' Diogenes endorsed her, fishing out some coins.

The boys ran up, serious but eager; they laid the nuts on the tarmac spiked one and slashed another open.

When asked, they answered that they were brothers; their eyes were round and brilliant, their thin and naked torsos and lanky limbs tensile in strength in spite of their spindliness. Barefoot, in faded cotton shorts, they both rubbed their noses on the heel of their free hands as Diogenes engaged them in talk. But on their side, it remained scanty; they danced a little on their feet.

Diogenes tipped up the pierced fruit and drank the liquid to the last drop, urging the journalist to do the same.

'Nectar,' he said, with a dramatic sigh of contentment. And he handed it back to the elder boy to be cut open for the 'jelly'. 'It's no good for the arteries, but if you could drink moonlight, it would look and taste like this.'

A jeep in camouflage paint passed them, swinging over to the wrong side of the road to overtake their parked car, then slowed, and started to reverse towards them fast.

'So, you boys, where's you getting that big bunch of coconuts?' The policeman poked at the younger boy. 'And you, hand me that machete now.'

'My auntie's tree …' The elder boy tossed his head slowly back towards the forest. 'In there.' He had no conviction, and the man shot back, 'And where in there might be your auntie's coconut grove?'

Mignonette was standing with a wedge of the perfumed, glistening fruit in her hand, frozen in the act of lifting it to her mouth; Larry Turner was midway through quaffing the lunar milk, and Diogenes Earle was reaching out to take another nut from one of the boys.

The officer went on, placing a hand on the boy's shoulder: 'We're taking you in.'

Another policeman, with a club stuck through his belt, swung down wide-legged from the jeep, lifted the bunch of greenish-yellow bearded fruits from the younger child, and hoisted them over his shoulder with a negligent finger.

'Officer,' began Diogenes, addressing the first policeman in his crisp uniform with his shiny leather straps and weapons. 'We're responsible. I have a visitor from Washington, DC, and we've been on a little sightseeing tour. We were thirsty. I merely wanted to treat him to one of our island's delicacies. The children fetched the cocos for us – at my request. I undertake to make sure everything is fine with the … their auntie.'

The second policeman was now pushing the bigger of the two youths towards the jeep.

'He's my younger brother …' the boy began protesting, twisting his head to look back at the child standing forlorn now on the verge. 'I can't leave him here.'

'So we'll take him in, too.'

Diogenes tried to look casual as he fished in his pocket, pulled out some ID and with it, some US greenbacks, folded underneath, which he slid out unconcernedly, moving closer to the first officer's gaze.

'You Dr Earle?' the man said, with a smile that had no smiling in it.

Diogenes nodded, fingering the money.

'We're proud of you.'

The officer threw a glance at the American, at the car, at Mignonette, and calling out to them, said, 'Dr Earle is an example of what this country can do.'

Diogenes saw that he'd mistaken his man: this one wanted to put on a show, play the big man with the big men. Perhaps the man was frightened the money would prove a trap, perhaps he was filled with unusual rectitude. 'Let me at least ...' Diogenes began. He wanted to say, 'Come with you to the station,' but the boys were already bundled into the back, their eyes staring through the panes in the doors that closed on them.

'We're not ashamed of this country,' said the policeman, as he secured the rear doors, and swung himself into the driver's seat.

Diogenes Earle put his wallet away.

In her flat later that evening, Mignonette was weeping for the boys; Diogenes had utterly failed to help, he'd let them fall into the hands of that vicious power freak ... It was all his fault; with him around, they'd been conspicuous, and that jeep was manned with the only officers on the whole island who wanted to show how the law was the law because of his fucking fame and that journalist from the *Post* who would have gone back home and said, Those islanders'll never change their spots. The boys were probably now lying battered and broken in some filthy cell, terrified out of their wits at what was still to come … She was sobbing, she was railing at him.

'Aren't you being a little melodramatic, my dear child?' said Diogenes. He had been about to take off his trousers. 'They'll give them a warning, and then they'll let them go.'

'That's what you say,' she said, passionately, turning her face into the mattress.

'Mignonette, my little one,' he began. He tried to stroke her, but she flinched and pushed her face harder into the mattress.

There was no staying with her longer that night, he could see.

'I will do something, I promise,' he said, letting himself out, with a glance back at the small, austere room.

He walked down the hill from her street to the Hilton, where he picked up a taxi. He asked the driver to take him to the Institute. The man was surprised: 'You work all hours, Dr Earle!'

It was nearly midnight.

He came in by the service entrance, reassuring the security guard with a squeeze on his shoulder.

In the lab's operating theatre, one monkey was lying on a bed, recuperating from surgery. Diogenes stroked the scant fur on the sleeping animal's belly and checked the screens on which her life systems pulsed in streams of stars.

'There, there, my beauty,' he murmured. 'You're doing fine.'

Then he put his face next to hers and smelled the mixture of antiseptic and animal heat in the residual warmth of her sleeping existence. Truly, she was all right, this creature with her slender black fingers crooked on her groin and her crinkled face with the lids beseechingly swollen over her eyes. There was another gurney lying empty alongside; Diogenes Earle climbed on to it and stretched out; the vervet being near, he was able to sleep.

MINK

'THE BEST MINK is blonde.' This was a favourite subject of our mother's. 'Darker mink – tawny or taupe – can be chic, but never gives quite the full effect – oh, the utter luxury of mink with a gold bloom on it, like an albicocca. Like a baby's bottom, like yours when you were babies!'

Donna Byrd, maiden name Sarto, wasn't like other mothers. Our mother! Even washing my father's socks in greying suds, wearing the heavy-duty rubber gloves she'd always put on to protect her hands, she was an exotic blow-in, and she radiated the warm south through the wind-whipped fens where we lived then. As she rubbed and wrung, her words spooled out bright ribbons of hopes for us. She was an expert dream-weaver, and we – that's me, Bea, for Beatrice, and my older sister, Ricky – short for Riccarda, because she was meant to be a boy – we jumped to catch them.

She smoothed her new perm off her cheek with the inner, soft edge of her forearm above the wet gloves, and went on: 'There are alternatives to mink: people swear by Canadian squirrel. But I don't go along with that at all. Margarine to butter. And don't you believe those advertisements. Margarine never tastes as good as butter.

'Now there is fox. Fox can be marvellous.' She closed her eyes and hummed to herself, nestling her head into an invisible corolla of fur around her shoulders, conjuring away the fenland drabness and carrying us off, far away. 'Ah, sable. Sable is unbelievably luxurious.' Her eyebrows were plucked into high arches and she flung back her head, to snuggle into the soft depths, with parted lips, like a film star on a poster. 'Sable comes from Russia,' she went on, 'like astrakhan. Russians are the Christian Diors of fur!

'And there's always ermine.'

Ermine! I saw queens and princes floating by, alighting on a mist-wreathed boat to sail, rudderless, across an enchanted lake towards a fairy palace on a spire-crowned island. They wore circlets round their brows, lined with ermine like the crown Elizabeth II wore at her coronation, the ceremony we bought our first family television set to watch.

If the Sunday roast had been a leg of lamb, Donna'd set us up to mince any leftovers. We'd clamp the clunky steel mangle to the kitchen table, and she'd pare off juicy bits near the bone and pass them to Ricky and me and tell us to watch out for our fingers as we fed the chunks into the funnel, taking turns on the handle to spin them out into fine threads of creamy pinkness. Next, we'd mash stale bread with milk and chop onion into the bowl with the ground lamb, and she'd add nutmeg and pepper and allspice and thyme and garlic, and we'd beat an egg at her instructions and stir it all in. Then we'd roll out the mixture on a floured board to pat into polpette to add to the tomato sauce for supper.

Fur came as trimmings, on cardigans and gloves, hats and collars and cuffs. She'd show us – in a copy of *Vogue*, which she always took – how a simple ruff or tippet or button or pompom lifted a nondescript outfit into a stratosphere of sophistication and allure. How a fur hat, especially one with a little voile scattered with moles like Marilyn's, added mystery to eyes looking out from under the brim.

This was power. I practised making eyes at myself in the mirror, dipping my head like a moorhen. When Ricky tried too, she just looked fierce. She has a temper and would knit her brows and hex you with her black eyes.

Donna Sarto wasn't going to settle for tassels or tippets. She scorned the way other women would be all smiles at a trifle – at a pair of mink earrings, for God's sake. She wanted a fur coat, one that enfolded her head to toe, that swung along under its own supple density as she stepped out.

She was saving up, and the laundry man helped, because she'd fill in the cheque each week for a little more than the bill, telling him she needed some cash.

Ricky and I hadn't really any direct experience of fur, not for real. My pink-eyed white mouse, known as Frosty, would slither through my fingers, warm and quivering; his coat was sparse over his rose-pale flesh and very soft and silky, and I pocketed him in my coat with the crumbs of biscuits there, and stroked him in secret.

'You could only make an elf's waistcoat from him,' said my mother, laughing, as she stitched nametags on to my school uniform sports shirts.

She handed over to me the latest *Vogue*. In the pictures inside there were fox furs that looked at you with liquorice eyes, and coats with paws hanging down.

She began swabbing off her nail polish. I liked the smell of the remover and sniffed it in. Then we heard my father come in back from work, and she quickly tidied away the manicure set.

'Don't mention the mink,' she said. 'I need to find the right moment.'

Our father wasn't having any of it.

'I've worn this suit for years!' He twisted around the label in the pocket on the inside lining to read the tailor's date ... 'Since 1946. That's a decade and it's as good as it ever was. You don't need a new coat, and you certainly don't need a stole. A stole is a silly bit of fluff, and it makes you look like one.' He struck a pose, sneering. Donna's lip trembled. I felt pricking in my eyes, not from shame at our mother wanting her mink but at my father for mocking her.

'Come on, old girl, don't get all worked up!' His tone changed – now he was making light of it. 'Think of it like this: minks are just rats, you know, but nastier.' He turned to us, to me, to enlist my support. He'd given up on appealing to Ricky because she never backed him up. 'Your mother doesn't realise Mrs Cranston isn't a patch on her. That woman can dress up to the nines all she wants in God knows what, mink or fish scales, for all I care, she'll never be a stunner. Com'n, you're a sensible little girl, tell your mother there's no need for one-upmanship.'

That was that, as far as he was concerned. The neighbour with the Jag, the swimming pool – and the mink – was flash, and flash was cheap.

Our mother stumbled on, her thin shoulders tensed. 'Mink is the warmest fur there is.'

'I seem to remember I bought you only the other day a very fine winter coat, made from the best Scottish dyed-in-the-wool tweed.' He was tapping his pocket, where he kept his wallet. 'That coat's got years in it still.'

How we minded her timorousness in face of his authority.

Ricky tried her best. Her eyes went all hexy, full and black, as she shouted at him, 'Everybody knows that mink is the best fur in the world and fur is much warmer than wool.'

'Ha ha,' he said. 'That's my fiery little woman! But don't believe what she tells you. Even if she is your mother, she's prone to believing all kinds of stuff and nonsense. Mark you, she's not as silly as some women. As that jumped-up Jennifer Cranston, for instance.'

Years later, Ricky told me, that this was the decisive moment for her. 'Bea, I understood then how we were going to have to have our own money. To do with it what we wanted. I was never going to be like our mother. I was never going to have to beg a man for anything I'd set my heart on.'

But Donna Sarto, our lively exotic mother, wasn't one to beg. She was like underground water, which is stronger than flames and molten magma; it grinds granite into fine sand and splits basalt, which is harder still.

Once we were at boarding school, she started squirrelling away more from the housekeeping. It took years – and it's another story, but also there was a friend, a friend who mended china, professionally, for antique dealers, and Donna learned from her how to spot a good piece at church sales.

She was able to put money aside, week by week.

I wasn't there the night she first came downstairs wearing her mink and took his arm to go out. But she told Ricky and me later how our father reacted.

'I say, old girl,' he spluttered, 'what's this?'

'He was awed, I'm telling you!' Donna'd remembered, purring with satisfaction. 'He couldn't imagine how I'd done it, and it felt wonderful. I tilted my head and lifted an eyebrow at him. You see, the whole pelt was flowing like silk all around me. I was Venus rising from the sea, Venus in furs!

'His glasses misted up so he drew out his arm from mine to take them off and wipe them.

'I'm telling you,' she added, laughing. 'I have never felt more feminine.'

The mink was in a plastic dress bag in the cupboard by the downstairs loo when I was at Donna's last house, clearing it out, three months ago. My sister and I were taking it in turns to go and sift through another room. I didn't know what was in the bag until I had unzipped it. It slumped through my hands, soft and supple, a bit chilled from its sojourn in the cupboard, and exuding naphthalene, which went up my nose. When I pulled it free and carried it into a stronger light I saw that in spite of the care Donna'd taken to keep it in the dark and the cold, it was rotting; the fur was falling off the skins like mange. I dared not look more closely; my hands felt itchy, as if some organisms were creeping from the fur on to my skin.

Throwing it away seemed the only thing to do. But it also seemed a terrible betrayal of Donna's carefully executed plot. Of the years involved. Of the triumphant conclusion.

I googled 'Recycling mink', and several sites came up. There was a cottage industry somewhere in Vermont where we could send Donna's fur coat and they would turn it into a luxury teddy bear or other soft toy.

Or there were charities, which sent old furs to refugee camps in Afghanistan and places during the bitter winters. The donations were tax deductible.

I emailed my sister about finding the coat, and she rang me, and we talked about it.

'There are also Fur Clinics,' she reported, 'where old coats are shown in class to raise consciousness. To pass on to the young a horror of wearing dead animals. Lou has friends involved. She'll send you the link.' Lou is her daughter, and an active eco-warrior.

'That seems a bit harsh,' I emailed Lou. 'It was a fashion, like ostrich feathers and crocodile handbags. Donna was a woman of her time. She couldn't have known otherwise. Not sure I want her up before the next generation to confess her crimes, even if she'll not be there in person.'

Then a friend told me she'd been through the same dilemma, with a mink stole of her mother's, and she'd found out that you could donate old furs to an animal welfare charity closer to home. It passed them on to farms for keeping orphaned nurslings warm, and it wouldn't matter about fleas or moths or mange.

Was this better?

Ricky and Lou thought so. We began to laugh, the thin, sad laughter that greets time's fell hand at work, because there's no other way to respond if you are to carry on living. All that glamour, nonchalance, and allure – that feminine mystique – Donna had pursued, turned into the lining of a nest for a newborn calf? Why not?

But in the end I did none of those things. I put the mink back in the bag and took it to the Recycling Centre and shunted it into a skip under the sign:

Miscellaneous Household Goods

(Penalty for Improper Use)

A RARE VISIT

In the flat in Cairo where we were living after World War II, there was a narrow mirror in the hall in a gilded frame; it was hung too high for me to look into, but I could watch my mother's face as she checked her reflection while the suffragi, Mohammed, went to open to the visitor who had pulled the little bell on its coil and made it dance and jingle. At the sound, Mohammed would glide across the cool polished floor in his soft babouches, his slight shadow cutting through the stripes of the shuttered twilight of our interior world. My mother, who by now had settled herself on the sofa in the drawing room, would then rise to greet her guest as if surprised, springing forward in a shimmer of tulle, her light shawl left drifting on the chintz soft covers and cushions. When she came to a standstill – she alighted, it seemed to me, as airy and luminous as my fairy doll – I'd catch hold of a bunch of fabric from her dress and steady myself to look from behind her at the new arrival: a stream of visitors would drop in during her 'hour' for tea in the afternoon when my father would still be at work. As often as not, they'd be there when he came home.

Calling out, 'Melissa, I'm home, it's a bloody dustbowl in town,' he'd stride into the drawing room, rubbing his hands.

'Had a good day, darling girl?' he'd ask, as he kissed my mother on the cheek. Then to me, he'd add, 'And what about you, little woman?' and swing me up in the air once, twice, three times even, and then set me down again and make straight for the drinks tray, shouting to Mohammed to bring a bucket of ice. My mother never joined him, but the guests did. They smoked too, my father keeping between his lips the flattened oval of the Egyptian cigarettes from Constantinou's (the Greek variety he favoured) as he bustled about, my mother's friends often preferring the Virginia tobacco brands that were kept in wood-lined silver boxes and passed round by Mohammed after he'd offered them from a brass tray, tumblers of gin and tonic and bitters, or other mixes of choice, as well as whisky and soda, or whisky and water.

My mother didn't smoke either. She'd sit quietly, her dress fanning out around her slender legs, while the guests ... well, the guests entertained her.

When her friend from her hometown came, I never made a peep, because I knew that if she remembered I was still there, she would send me away. Zio Folco – he had a very fancy name, with a title from Italy as well as some high military rank – was a decorated veteran of both world wars, and in the partigiani, too, my mother would emphasise, and he arrived sometimes in riding gear, sometimes in civvies, sometimes even in Arab dress, which I loved to see – for he'd come riding in from the desert to the west of Cairo. He was living there with the local Bedouin, and he would only ever drink mint tea – 'With five sugars, remember!' he'd remind Mohammed in Arabic – and he'd sit beside my mother on the sofa. He would talk, and she would cry.

That afternoon in 1951, he reported, 'Melissa, I have been looking now for three years in the dunes, and we have so far uncovered the unmarked resting places of one and a half thousand Italians, and nearly three hundred others of every flag, including Allies from Eighth Army, your esteemed husband's fellow soldiers. But besides these – may they rest in peace at last – we have unearthed at El Alamein, among the debris of battle, the rusted tanks and shells, the unexploded mines and live ammunition still buried there, where it was abandoned – we have dug up heaps and heaps of unidentified bones ... The desert took their owners, more than a thousand who have no names – but the desert is merciful and the conditions have preserved these remains. God willing, with patience and pains we shall identify more of these sacrificed heroes – from all sides, regardless of nation.

'I shall not give up, Melissa. Not until I have tracked every trackless waste in that heaving dry sea of sand ...'

'But the mines, Folco!' my mother would murmur. 'The mines are so ...'

He would take her hand and kiss it, and finish her phrase.

'Perilous, I know. But don't be anxious. My trackers, my men, the local people of the desert, they have a sixth sense, dear beautiful lady! But alas, we have lost some of them – six have died in this great endeavour.

'This is our great work!'

On this occasion, he brought the first plans for the mausoleum he was building at El Alamein, and spread them out on the coffee table to show her. My mother was poring over them with him, and he was kneeling beside her on the floor on one knee, pointing to this and that, when the front door sounded, and in came my father, and cried out,

'To what do we owe the pleasure of this rare visit?'

And Folco leaped up, and shook my father's hand warmly, and began showing him the plans too, and soon they were both talking very loudly at once.

That night I heard my mother crying in their bedroom. Later, when I was older, I would learn that my father's greatest, most painful jealousy rose when she saw people from Italy; it filled him with fear that he, her husband, who had rescued her from her country at its lowest ebb, would be shut out of her innermost life.

When I heard her crying, I would creep in to be with both of them in their bed, because she would stop then, for my sake, I knew.

Sometimes, though, it sounded too loud to interrupt.

That same night, several soldiers were roaming around my bed, taking up positions at the foot and by the sides, and they would not go away even when I pulled the sheet over my head and wished them away through my fairy doll. I thought my mother was crying that night because they were coming into her room too, and I ran through their ranks out of mine, holding on to my doll for a shield, whispering that she must do some magic to send them away so they could be found by Folco in the sand and kept buried for good in his shrine.

SING FOR ME

Solitudinem faciunt pacem appellant
(They make a desert and call it peace)
Tacitus

I n those days the rumour started that there would be an inquiry. Full and frank disclosure, the government kept hinting. A tribunal of independent adjudicators and observers. Independent observers. They'd look into the events thoroughly. And into the sequence of events that led to them, into the decisions and actions that led to those particular events on that day.

The correct name for what happened was 'Operation Light of Day'. That was what the history books will call it. But my husband, the Captain Procurator, always referred to it as 'the manoeuvres'. I used to say 'the mistake' (but I avoided talking about it, then, and I still don't like to dwell on it now). Maia, she called those events 'the outrage'.

I so wished she wouldn't.

An inquiry had been going on all along, of course – beneath the surface. Not yet officially. But questions were the stuff we breathed. Except that we didn't breathe.

At home, Maia might as well not have been there. She was always in her room, on her machine, writing, writing. When she did talk to me, she'd argue, 'We have to find out. So that there won't be a next time. So that it stops. Any progress towards peace has to start by finding out who did it, and what exactly they did. How many people? How many died?'

But my husband, he wouldn't see it that way. He'd ruminate. 'Robust, full, frank disclosure? Transparency? Yes, of course.' But then he'd start qualifying this and qualifying that, and Maia would get angry with her father till he'd say to her, 'That's what we're told. That self-examination's the gold standard of democracy. That is what the government wants, and we agree. I agree. Every nation on this earth should be accountable and transparent. Absolutely.

'But there's a limit to all this ... fessing up. Some things should be known, but some things not. Some things should be said, but some things – I told them, no way will I give the inquiry the go-ahead here.'

For the people who lived there, in that place where the mistake happened, the events are known by the name of the place that was once their home: a somewhere of little importance till then, a place nobody in their right mind would have wanted to go, let alone live. Until the mistake put it on the map, you could say, and the world's media descended on it.

By then there wasn't much of it left at all. Though now there is ... a bit more. It's being rebuilt by our forces, with help from NGOs, of course.

I say 'we' ... but I'm speaking for myself. My husband, the Captain Procurator, he didn't agree. He had responsibilities for so many things. And then he had decisions to make about the inquiry too. Whether it was to come here. And if it did, who'd be allowed to attend. How much funding it'd be allotted. And who'd be called to give evidence …

Would he be called? Or would he be allowed only to preside? To stay in charge?

When they took place – the events in that small place – he was much younger. He was acting under orders from men – and women – higher in rank than him.

It was a long time ago.

He would say to us, 'It depends who's doing the remembering and of what, doesn't it? History matters, but who the historians are matters more. I always ask, who's telling this story? Whose voice am I hearing? Do I want to listen to other people's stories? To throw good money after *their* stories? I know what they say about the manoeuvres. I know what they'll want to say. What about their constant low-grade shelling, their endless attacks on us? Haven't we suffered ten times, a hundred times more?

'For as long if not longer?

'Besides, many other things have happened since. Terrible things. We were at war, for God's sake. We were making the peace.'

Our daughter, Maia, has always been a good student – straight As since she was first at school – but she decided very young that she wanted to be a musician. She used to play classical music, piano pieces. Lovely stuff – and difficult. She could always sing, too. And when she was a little girl, we used to hear her sing. She'd look blissful, singing, she loved it. You could see the music pick her up on its waves. It made her fly away inside, she said.

But then she joined a band, and they gadded about, doing gigs at parties. They were always staying out late. She'd wince and chew her hair when I used to say she'd go deaf with the loudness, and that would be the end of a musical career. But she'd almost spit at me, and I didn't know what to say to her when she'd got that mood on her. She was fourteen years old and she already had worry lines between her brows. If I tried to smooth them with my fingers she'd snap at me, that she didn't care. 'You put them there,' she said. 'Ugly suits me,' she said. 'Ugly suits you.'

She used to make me cry.

That was when she took to calling the events the outrage. Just like they did, the ones who are bombing us in the streets, dropping devices in our shopping baskets and under our bus seats.

My husband, the Captain Procurator, he was getting angry, too. He'd rail against the government: the peace process was turning every one of our leaders into … '*therapists* …' We're all to line up and lie down, while they bang on about 'truth recovery' and 'forgetting leads to festering' and 'remembering is healing'. Bahh. How we've got to become a 'holistic society'. Naww.

'Some things should be remembered,' he'd say. 'But the rest. Just causes trouble. Reopening wounds. Salting them.'

At first Maia pleaded with him. She'd say, 'We have to live differently.'

But the danger signs really began for me when she was about to turn fifteen. It was two years ago, and she'd promised to be home and we'd celebrate, a family together. I asked her to sing.

But when it came to the moment, she wouldn't, she ran out of the room, screaming at us. How she hated us, how we filled the world with slime.

I've tried to unpick what happened to her: you know, like an Indian scout, putting my ear to the railway tracks to catch the distant vibrations.

I suppose the first faint tremors I caught began when she was smaller, and she began to ask questions if we were together, watching the news. Her father always answered her: 'So who's the bright one in this family?' he'd say. He was so proud of her. '*You*. And you're right to ask about what is happening. I'll explain. Explain everything. Killing is always regrettable but it's not always wrong. God says so: it is in the Scriptures that it's right to exterminate enemies who are bent on exterminating you. It's even more justified when that enemy is bent on destroying you by any means, however ruthless. *They* have shown us on every occasion that they'll stop at nothing. Not even at the death of innocent victims. Innocents like you. You're in danger, my darling girl, you and all your little friends and their friends.

'I've always done everything I can, God knows, to protect you and I shall always do so.'

In those days she was scared for him. When he was away on a tour of duty she'd be looking at the news, chewing her hair. She didn't want him to be there, wherever it was, doing whatever he did. He wasn't in the fighting any more but though she knew that, she was still frightened her daddy would die. Not, then, that he'd be the one who ...

Sometimes, when he was back from a tour, we'd be watching the news together, and she'd be frowning and scowling and he'd try to cheer her up and coax her to give him a little smile, a nice smile for her Daddy. But then, she started not coming down when we were going to have dinner. She wasn't hungry. I'd go and knock at her bedroom door. She'd started making us knock at her door. And she'd call back without moving, 'I need to be private.' I'd hear the sound of a click, and then that tootle, you know, when the laptop closes down. Sometimes it was her phone she'd snap shut. I'd go down again and her father would start railing at me, as if it was my fault, saying it was dinner time and this family had its meals together like a proper family, at seven o'clock punctually, and how he wanted her to bring friends home, they were all welcome.

Then, one day when she was at school, I went into her room. I am her mother and I need to watch out for her, so I told myself that there was no reason to feel badly about snooping on her, with all that coming and going and late nights … I had every cause for concern.

There it was, on her screen, some kind of blog she was writing under a strange name. 'Bring friends home! To meet my father? He used to show me his campaign medals; he used to stand to attention and march up and down while I stood up in my nappies and clapped him and gurgled. He's shown me that home video, over and over. Sometimes he'd take his gun out of the locked cupboard in his study and hand it to me to feel its weight – and its cold. Or he'd get his sidearm out of its holster and tip out the bullets and then spin the chamber and give it to me to hold while it was spinning – and it was warm from his hands and you could see how he loved it, loved his gun.'

Oh God, when I saw what she was up to. The shaking on the tracks – I could read it now.

We should've seen it coming. No, that's not right. *I* should have seen it coming. I did. But I didn't admit it to myself. I couldn't, not then. It was unimaginable. Though her actions were by no means isolated. She was part of a trend. A movement, *they* called it. They wanted openness, truth, they said. She was writing to her friends, 'There've been inquiries in other places, they make it possible to move on. We know lots now. We know what they don't tell us ... They do things and they don't think about what they do. What it means for us who have to live with the outrage.

'*Make wars history!*'

The threads, long, long threads with little postage-stamp faces beside them. Of her friends. Dozens of them. Some I did know. Her friends in the band. And they were talking to *them* too. Exchanging bulletins about what happened and what is happening. They were organising.

'They've made us complicit,' she wrote. 'And we're not the ones whose homes have been ransacked and wrecked and demolished, the innocent who've been shot and killed. We're still alive. I live here, in this fine house, the house of the Captain Procurator, and I have a room all to myself, and all the food I need and water. Water whenever I want it. Hot and cold.'

I was really frightened. What *he* would do if he knew. That she could be the one who gets hurt. I was trembling. But something in me was excited, too.

It was a few days later, and we were watching the news – or rather, Maia was watching, with me. We were quiet, together, even happy. The Captain Procurator wasn't home – he was on a mission ... And the newsreader began announcing that new evidence had been made available about Operation Light of Day – the manoeuvres, the mistake. On April 12 that terrible year thirteen years ago.

I was really frightened. What he would do if he knew. That she could be the one who gets hurt.

And we saw him. He was – facing a man who was waving his hands in the air. I wasn't sure. No, that's not it. I wanted not to be sure. And she … well, when she was a little girl, she used to squeal with the thrill of it, when she glimpsed her father in the gunship, sitting in the tail with his machine gun between his knees, or when he was talking to camera after an operation. Now, though, I could see she knew that even though he was so much younger it was still her father in the shot, he was the man with the gun, and he's holding it in the face of an old man, who's waving both his hands in the air and his hands are empty. The Captain – my husband – is younger and the film's jumpy and a bit fuzzy. But it's him.

He came back and he said to her, 'It'll be my birthday soon. I'm going to be forty-five years old. Forty-five. An old man!

'I want you to do something for me.' His voice was soft and kind. 'The day you were born, I was away. I heard the news on the phone in the camp. I remember I cried. I cried, I did.

'Go on, cheer up your old father on his birthday. Sing something for me! You used to sing. You sing so nicely when you want to. Sing for me. An old song, a song I remember from when I was your age. That way I'll feel young again.'

She was smiling, she was playing to his tune, and for a moment, I was tranquil, we were going to be a family again.

She said, 'And if I sing, Father, will you give me something I really want?'

'Of course,' he said. 'Anything. I swear, by everything that's holy.' He was laughing, and he would have given her the moon and the stars. But he offered her a car, an iPod, you name it, but she was shaking her head, still smiling. 'No, nothing like that,' she said. 'I want something instead that means something – to you, to us all.'

'That's my girl!'

He was beaming.

I could feel her fierceness, like a rip tide rising, and he was in the water and he didn't know it.

I felt a hollow under my ribs, and a bird caged there flew up and out – and I was holding on to her arm, my daughter's arm, and walking with her towards him, and I didn't let go but squeezed her and felt how thin her whole frame is – my daughter's body, so thin – when she went up to him and she put her hand in his and told him he had to testify.

When Maia comes to see me now she gives me courage. She says, 'If you cut yourself out of the process of inquiring into what happened and what is still happening, if you refuse to know what we did and how we did it, tomorrow will be an alien place and this country where we live will become a desert.'

I warm myself at her fire.

'Daddy did right to confess, he knows he did. Even the judge at the tribunal agreed that he was trying to be a good man and do his duty.'

She tells me, 'We're all connected. There is no *Them*. "Because others are, I am; I am because you are."' She's quoting, she tells me, from a poet, a poet far away. 'We couldn't go on living like that, hardly daring to draw breath in case we let something slip.'

When she speaks like that, when my daughter speaks, it is as if she's inside me, voicing my trapped soul. I feel it flutter like a bird trying out its wings. That a child should give breath to the parent, isn't that against nature?

BREADCRUMBS

THE MOON WAS up higher in the sky than she'd sailed since … oh, a long time ago and I could see her through the crooked blind sliced into pieces and falling in stripes like Blake's tiger turned silver bright no longer daylight golden across my bed in Room 9.12 where I was lying with white and luminous fluids dripping into me from upside-down vessels like fishing floats; I was in their net, scooped up from the lower depths. Being saved from drowning wasn't altogether comfortable, but it wasn't the moon keeping me awake. The awkwardness of being tethered in the net of those feeds and liquids slithering into me made blissful, dreamless sleep elusive, and besides, the moon was rousing others and I could hear them at the nurses' station, murmuring to one another and now and then giving a quick laugh or a snort.

It was the same every night – they chatted and hobnobbed and told tales to get through the shift. But this time it was different, the moon was soaring and she was carrying us, the doctors and the nurses on night duty in their pools of light by their monitors, the orderlies and the ambulance drivers in the sumps down below waiting a call and the medics and surgeons and police officers in A&E looking out for the stabbers and the stabbed, the gunshot wounds and their makers, and me suspended in my high computerised net of a bed, she was carrying all of us somewhere.

The night-duty doctor had finished ribbing Grace the nurse from Ghana about her love of lemongrass chicken soup and pad thai which were her favourite foods that she dreamed of and couldn't get in this damned hospital which had every ECG and MRI and CGI machine you could think of but no kitchen or cafeteria for a hungry nurse at night and then the youngest of the team who was from Bangalore and had very gentle tiny fingers like a clever daughter in a fairy tale broke through their chaffing and asked Grace how she'd arrived in this country in the first place and got such a taste for spicy exotic cuisine here and Grace laughed and said, 'You're not supposed to ask that kind of question, you know! You're not meant to think I don't belong here! Who's to say my granddaddy didn't live here a hundred years ago?'

Then another voice broke in and whispered, 'I'll tell you how I came here ...' and I could hear her even though she was speaking softly because the others all fell silent around her and the moonlight stretched out silver cool and taut over them so that her voice travelled towards me like music over water in the summer in a park at dusk and she was saying, 'Every day there were soldiers and explosions and aeroplanes overhead. We still got our children to school, through the checkpoints and the rest of it. But one day when they went to school, the explosions were coming in closer. We were used to it, but ...'

She was speaking quietly, with a kind of detachment.

'Yes, that day the soldiers came and I lost my children. The men came running in to our house; one had the traditional scarf tied round his head so you couldn't see his face. He was followed by another man, who had his scarf half pulled off so we could see his eyes all startled and hot in his head.'

Her voice was changing, becoming deeper and older.

'They waved us out of our house with their guns, they pointed down the street, away from the direction of the school. We tried to stand up to them and stay where we were, we tried to dodge them and run to fetch the children but they howled the troops were out there on the attack, house to house. Everyone was shouting. Running and screaming and the smell of bombs everywhere. You never see that smell on the news or the smell that comes with it – like here in hospital … sometimes down in surgery. Insides. The smell of hurt animals. Blood and flesh and fire.

'You know all this.'

There was a murmur from the others.

I heard a voice – it was Grace's, saying, 'Maryam, when did this happen? How long ago?'

A bell rang from one of the beds … Ahmad the night-duty doctor who was from Libya broke in, you could hear he wanted to know, 'Hey, don't get to the end before I'm back …'

But Maryam went on, 'We women who'd been rounded up spent that first night together, in an old garage for bus repairs, and in the morning when the soldiers marched us to a camp and told us all to look for our families and our children and regroup, I didn't find Raja and Leila. Many of the others with us had got separated too. It went on like this, for one day and night after another. It seemed the longest time. Wherever we were taken, I asked about them, the others asked about theirs. Sometimes someone found their mother, but for us there was no word, just a huge silence in the middle of the explosions of the bombs and the rumble of the artillery outside and the endless wailing inside us. It's hard to think of ways of describing children so that someone might recognise them – what do you say? My son is six, he has dark curly hair … my daughter is eight, she's so pretty your heart melts, and she has a chip on her first front tooth from falling over as she was running one afternoon?

'They were lost. I had lost them. Or had I gone missing? Had our lives left us and walked away? Had we all somehow gone missing?

'We were kept moving, drawing farther and farther away from our home and our street and the school where they were going when I last saw them.

'One lunchtime, on the eighth day it was, I had to show my ID as usual to one of the guards and it was then I had the idea.

'From that day on, I tore up my face in little pieces – first one eye then the other, then the mouth, one corner then the other, then the nose and the hair, and I left the bits behind me in the places they turned into holding camps for us, I left a bit with anyone who would go along with my doing this and take it. It was one of the medical volunteers who pinned a piece to his own badge that my Leila saw. She was lining up for an inspection and she said to Raja – she had kept a strong grip on him – "Look there's Mother – that's Mother's eye …"

'That way we found one another again. It took another five days but we were re-united. After that terrible gap, a gap like an eternity.'

It was the time again for the moon to start sliding down the sky. The tiger stripes across my bed were contracting and fading, and I was feeling drowsier now, as I heard Grace and the others at the nurses' station sigh and kind of chuckle with satisfaction. 'But you still haven't explained how you got here afterwards, darling,' I heard Grace say, banteringly.

'That will have to keep for another night,' said Ahmad, yawning. 'Nearly time for the day shift to come on. Are you on tomorrow, Maryam?'

But there was no reply. Or else I was too near sleep to hear.

THE DIFFERENCE IN THE DOSE

'OTHER CHILDREN HAVE a nonna,' says Daisy. 'Why not me?' She turns her face up to her mother, who is combing her hair after washing it. It is curly and thick and tangles easily, so Bella combs it through before Daisy goes to bed, where she will wake the next morning with her hair in fiery spikes again. Bella's full name is Belladonna, the name of another flower, a different kind from lilies or roses, daisies or buttercups.

A flower that can be good for you, sometimes.

Bella's own mother understood plants, and belladonna had a special significance for her, she used to say. She was a herbalist, she knew these things. She liked to quote, 'The only difference between a poison and a remedy is the dose.'

Daisy is plucking at Bella's sleeve; she insists, her mouth beginning to twist into a cry, 'Everyone in my class has a nonna. I'm.The.Only.One.Who.Hasn't.' She spells out each word as if learning to pronounce it for the first time.

'Your granny ...' Bella hesitates. Then she says, 'Let me tell you a story, which will explain everything.'

And she begins:

'Women sometimes discover they are having a baby only because they have a sudden craving. In Italian this urge is called, simply, la voglia. The want. The same word as "will", but with the definite article added: *the* want. That makes it much more absolute. We call it a craving. When I was small, my mother told me, la voglia is irresistible. It's a force that takes over and makes you ... quite irrational, quite uncontrollable. When la voglia comes over her, the future mother won't be refused. She'll stop at nothing – do you realise? – to get what she needs.

'*Needs?* Maybe. But maybe the substances she craves aren't helpful to the new life inside her ... Or maybe they're just caprices, the aberrant fancies of a mind unbalanced by endocrinal surges ...'

She's rushing on, talking to herself, she realises; she has lost the little girl's attention. So she changes direction, forgets the technical stuff, and says, 'We might want all sorts of crazy things when someone like you is waiting to be born. Some not so crazy too. Our cravings can be an excuse for

    chocolate truffles

    lavender pastilles

    fried chips in strawberry jam

    ice cream galore – pistachio, rum truffle, tutti frutti,

    raspberry swirl, coconut candy, or any flavour you can

    think of. Häagen-Dazs Dulce de Leche Mini-cups...!'

'Cherrimisù!' cries Daisy.

'In some places they can all be bought in the middle of the night – imagine! Like a pizza, you can get them delivered!'

There's a pause as both picture this craziness. Then her mother goes on: 'In some cases we want other things, we want:

    coal dust from the scuttle

    the colouring bits inside crayons

    mud and silt from puddles in the road

mustard and horseradish and ginger
soap powder and shampoo
beetles and eggshells
and ...'

She starts laughing.

Daisy giggles too. She begins to look around the room.

'Carpet,' she shouts. 'You might want to eat carpet!' She bangs on the table. 'And wood! Nice tasty wood!'

'No,' says the child's father, when he comes in and hears the stories his wife's telling their daughter. 'No, those things would harm the baby inside.'

He goes to the fridge and brings out a bottle of white wine and begins to look for the corkscrew.

'Wine is bad for embryos,' he says.

'But it wasn't when I was having you,' says Bella to her daughter, cross with Piero because he has broken into their game. 'And look at you, nothing wrong with you!'

The father pours out a glass for himself and another for Bella; Daisy settles herself against her mother and begins to draw with her finger in the misty veil forming on the bowl. Bella strokes her hair, which is almost dry now after her bath.

'Your nonna had cravings when she was having me.'

Daisy looks up at her with excitement.

'What for?'

'Oh ... spinach and carrots and things. Parsnips!' says Piero, her father, and leans over and kisses Bella firmly, to change the subject.

'Parsnips,' giggles Daisy, and makes a face.

'She ate them raw!'

He grinds and snaps his teeth at Daisy, not to fail the general mood of jollity, because he realises how heavy he's been. But he can't help it, and adds, 'That's how weird women get.'

Belladonna can't remember her birth mother, the mother who had the cravings. She wouldn't ever have been able to remember her, because she was a tiny baby, only a few weeks old, when she was adopted, and she was never shown a photograph of her by the mother she knew, the one who brought her up, Charis Merryll, the beautiful lady gardener, best-selling author of several classic titles (*Orchids in the Penthouse*; *Urban Plots*; *Hanging Gardens for the Mostly Manicured* – and her most famous of all, *The Difference in the Dose*).

It's been ten years since Bella quarrelled with Charis, a little longer than the length of time since Daisy was born. Charis found out that Bella was sleeping with Piero; she found them together in bed, in *her* bed, the one with the satin canopy bunched up into a cherub's fist, which was such bliss to sleep under. Charis was back from somewhere a day earlier than expected, and she'd come whooping into the lobby of the apartment block where they lived, thinking how it was so great – she'd finished the assignment ahead of time, and now she and her daughter could have a precious day together over the weekend, something that didn't happen often enough, something she treasured, better than usual weekend quality time, real time out from her busy life planning and planting gardens all over the world for architects, bringing greenery to the desert for hotels in the Gulf, and turning into new Edens the oil-rich Emirates' island utopias which were rising up out of the swirling salt barrenness.

Charis was thinking all of this as she greeted the doorman of her Madison Avenue apartment block, the Golden Tower, as she went up in the elevator to the penthouse floor, as she pushed at the door, which was never locked, and found that it was, surprisingly, shut and bolted.

'Bella!' she cried out at the door. She never carried keys; she didn't need them, because the doorman and the janitor kept the tower quite safe.

'Bella!' Her heart contracted. Charis knew then something was wrong, terribly wrong.

She saw her child in peril. Images of horror jumped in her mind; interference storms jangled the stream of pixels from some terrible news bulletin: Bella sprawling, Bella drugged, Bella drunk, Bella damaged, abducted, gang-raped, murdered.

The screaming inside her was already beginning as she went down again in the elevator to fetch the doorman to let her into her own home.

She was shaking as she asked him for his keys, and she didn't conceal her agitation from him. She was forming a different picture from her first terrors as she registered, with hindsight, that he had greeted her with a degree of surprise that was perhaps unexpected.

'Oh, you're back so early, Ms Merryll,' he'd said, before he had added, with his more customary courtesy, 'Have you had a good trip this time?'

Going back up in the elevator, her sense of ominousness gathered. The doorman opened the service door at the back, the one they never used, and she entered her apartment through the kitchen, and began taking in the trail of tumbled glasses and dishes, the mulchy cocktail of smoke and booze and pizza, the drawn curtains and dropped blinds, the cushions tossed this way and that on the floor, the furniture moved out to the edges of the room, one lot of bodies sprawled on the couch, fast asleep, another heap of tangled limbs on the divan, the garden room window opened, her precious plants exposed to the night air. She started in her rage towards her daughter's bedroom: there she found more kids. Yes, kids, girls from Bella's class. Boys, too. She pulled off the covers to see where her daughter was. Not there. Not in the living room. She then realised, before she threw open the door to her own bedroom, where she would be.

She pulled off the sheets – and she saw Piero flung down on his front with nothing on – though she didn't yet know who he was. She saw only a man, a fully grown man with hair on his legs and his buttocks, too, and even on his back, an old man. Then she recognised him: one of her circle of friends, a man she knew, a successful businessman with a string of wig makers, costumiers, and hire shops, a man almost her own age, someone she had found amusing, pleasant, clever at business, but not, absolutely not … not for her child, not like this, not to sleep with her. Rage began breaking her open, letting fly a swarm of demons.

He was lying with one arm over the body of her daughter. His right hand was plunged into her hair, and she was still in a party dress – and one of her own best outfits, Charis realised – though it was all undone and messed up around her. So without even knowing what she was doing, she grasped him by the shoulder and began hitting him as the tears started pouring down. He sprang up and hit her back, square on her left cheek with his right hand, and he was a vigorous man who weighed at least two stone more than Charis, and his blow sent her reeling to the floor.

Bella was awake now, screaming at them both, standing up in her mother's muddled dress, her hair bunched and knotted and sticking out in all directions.

'You don't deserve Bella,' Piero was shouting. 'You're a dried-up old bitch, and all your mothering is a big fucking lie.'

'Che stronza,' he bawled at her as he tied the sheet around himself like a smart beach sarong. 'You've only ever wanted your big career and your big fucking credit card – you don't know anything about being a mother. Well, I love Bella. I am mother and father and lover and husband to her. I love her in ways your sort can never understand.'

They raged at each other. And Bella took his side. Bella turned on her, said unheard-of terrible things to her, poured out a pent-up hatred on her, which, it seemed, had been harbouring for years and years.

'You took me from my family. You stole me from my real mother. You thought you could buy me. Well, I am not someone you can buy. Not any more. I am not a slave.'

Piero put his arm around her and tucked her in under his high shoulder, fastening her to him as if she were now his baby.

'Bella loves me,' he said. 'I am the best thing that ever happened to her. I love her more than you ever could. You selfish old bag, you wanted a trophy child. Another lifestyle accessory.

'Well, it's over. It's my turn now.

'You can buy yourself a puppy.'

Charis was thinking:

In those days, I was so hoping for a child. The streets seemed to me to be crowded with nothing but women displaying their bumps, their navels pertly stuck out like a nipple, the parks teeming with young mothers with Walkmans dangling from their ears, pushing strollers, sometimes speeding on roller blades or, if the kids were a little older, sitting in the sun together chatting – by the playgrounds or the soccer pitch or the ice rink, where their offspring would be running about learning to be social.

But I, I had had abortions in earlier days when it seemed that every time I went to bed with someone it happened, even if I was doing everything to prevent it. Then, when I wanted to have a baby, when I had established my business and had the books done and dusted and everyone wanted a Charis Merryll low-maintenance urban plot with every remedy and every herb you need, it stopped happening.

Alfred couldn't take my wanting one so much – it wore him out, my crying. It cut him out.

So I thought, I will find someone who is like I was then, someone who can have a baby very easily and then have another soon so won't miss the first one, and I'll persuade her to give me hers.

My plot – a different kind of plot – was quite clever, though I say so myself.

At the noise of the fight in the main bedroom the rest of the party began to stir, though not all of them. Some roused themselves and padded about in the apartment, trying to shake their lethargy and their hangovers and find their clothes and other belongings to make a getaway.

Gradually, the others woke up, too, as their friends gave them warning prods. At last, Charis was alone with her daughter and her daughter's boyfriend, the man old enough to be her father.

'She is *seventeen*,' said Charis. 'And you, how old are you? Forty?' She'd spat out the word.

'I'm old enough to get married,' cried Bella. 'My mother was my age when I was born. You told me so yourself. And Piero loves me, he says so. We're going to go and live far away from here, far away from you.'

Weariness set in quickly. Charis was soon begging them to forgive and forget, as she would do, she promised. She'd experienced a terrible shock, but they could both work through it with time – and with love. They should live with her, or at least near her.

She was grubby with tears; she knew she couldn't command Bella's love exclusively. She had to let go. But not now, not yet.

Piero had taken Bella with him to Italy, where they were now living; Charis had tried to prevent him by making Bella a ward of court, but he pre-empted her legal moves, and true to what he had sworn that terrible night ten years ago, he indeed married Bella on her eighteenth birthday, the day of her majority, when Charis could no longer exercise any jurisdiction over her daughter. Except love, and her love no longer equalled his in her daughter's needs.

Since then, Charis's letters have had no answer, and there is no point in her trying to telephone, since her calls to their mobiles are blocked, and in the house and in his offices Piero employs staff, and the staff have instructions not to take calls from Charis.

Yet Charis still moves through Bella's dreams, though

she never tells Piero, because he always falls into a rage at the thought of her. Charis also appears to Bella by day: even though they are living far from Manhattan, where Charis still lives, Bella in Italy sees her mother's quick step in someone crossing a street in front of her, or in the lithe contours of a figure in the crowd passing by on the television in the background of some event. But it's an illusion; in fact they have not seen one another since that morning when Piero gathered her up with a few scraps of her things and planned everything – the honeymoon in Venice, the house in the hills outside Siena, and then the old palazzone in the country near Milan, where he had inherited from his dead parents an apartment with cracked frescoes on the high walls that told ancient stories of the gods, how they changed shape to make love to human girls who struggled to escape: changing their form, turning into trees, rivers, animals, flowers – and stars.

Then Daisy was born.

Daisy is ten years old now and she wants to know her granny.

'How much do you love me?' Daisy asks Bella. 'Show me!' She holds her arms out wide. 'I love you this much.' She retracts them a little bit: 'And I love Pappi this much.'

'And I love you this much!' Bella imitates her daughter, throws her arms out as wide as she can and then brings them together around her and squeezes her tight.

Daisy gurgles and wriggles and squeals.

'It's too tight, you're crushing me too tight!'

Bella lets her go.

When she was a child, Bella began to realise that some of the other kids she knew had a father, and she only had a mother, and her mother was old, old enough to be her grandmother, or the mother of her school friends' mothers. Charis could look all haggard and witchy at the school gates, with her long white hair in a frizz and her dungarees and her grimy fingernails, so Bella ordered her not to come and stand near the exit but some way off, if she insisted on coming at all.

But once she began to pester Charis with questions, Charis told her that her birth mother had not been able to keep her, because she was ill and poor and tired; that she had wanted Bella to have a better life than she could give her, and had loved her too much not to want the very best for her.

But Charis never told Bella how it had come about; how she had plotted long and hard, how her need had rendered her lucid, rational, and resolute; how she had persevered, examining and re-examining the situation until the right candidate turned up, and she knew she had found the right woman to be the mother of the child that was going to be hers.

First Charis had taken the idea for the book to her agent, and then the agent had submitted the plan to a publisher, the right enterprising young publisher for such a strong marketing idea, one that combined so neatly two best-selling lines, 'Gardening' and 'Mind Body Spirit'. Then, with the advance, Charis had leased a waste ground between two buildings on the Upper East Side in Spanish Harlem and brought in tons of earth to plant her Well Woman's Garden. Herbs and spices, teas and berries, flowers and bushes with properties that eased menstrual cramps and regulated cycles, that sweetened tension and lightened moods, softened skin and strengthened nipples of nursing mothers; her garden had different geographical zones, some under cloches and glass frames to protect them against the New York frosts, some inside in two conservatories warmed by bulbs that glowed in the night like cat's eyes.

She studied monks' herbals and Caribbean wise women's manuals; she consulted the local curanderas from San Domingo and Dominica in the neighbourhood and travelled to Guada-lajara and Mexico City to talk to the stall holders in the street markets there who sold remedies in coloured twists of paper.

In the Well Woman's Garden she planted saffron crocus and the spiky aloe; jojoba and echinacea; all the familiar cu-linary herbs and some not so familiar – alongside rosemary and parsley grew tansy and lovage and comfrey and sorrel and scabious. She scattered seeds of evening primrose by the wall facing west as the yellow trumpets drank in sunshine, and planted henbane in the crannies where it would cling to crumbs of earth. Queen Anne's lace, foxgloves, poppies were to grow wild, as if in a meadow.

All her plants were common, and all of them could be used to poison – as well as to heal.

She was greening the granite city.

In the more formal beds, she planted belladonna and vervain, rampion and rue – this was the part of the garden that was especially concerned with gynaecological troubles. She watched rampion begin to follow its name and climb vigor-ously up the wicker obelisks she provided: this was the king's cure-all, one of the most versatile of helpers, with a profound sway over the menstrual cycle. It was only one emmenagogue among several others: botany tuned in to biology. After all, plants were not so far from humans in their metabolism and their chemistry. Charis herself always felt brighter on clear days, and low cloud overhead made her droop.

The bed where belladonna and rampion grew was the part of the garden that was the heart of the project: her book *The Difference in the Dose* focussed on the principle that Charis had gleaned from the great Swiss physician Paracelsus, that sometimes the distance between boon and bane, between remedy and poison, between a comfortable pregnancy and a miscarriage, is a simple matter of a level teaspoon or a heaped one.

This part of the garden was controversial; rumours spread on the street (and Charis did nothing to discourage them) that what she grew there had power over babies growing in the womb.

She had assistants; she had sonar sensors to alert the presence of intruders, and a guard on duty at night as well.

Bella's mother was one of the visitors who came by one day, as others had done before her, and began to ask about the garden and that particular patch. She needed help, she said, help with morning sickness, which was making her life a torment. Charis saw her and understood her, felt the mixed fears of a young girl who was having a baby she hadn't thought to have, not yet, not now, and craved a medicine. Charis offered her an alternative, and as they talked, Charis recognised that at last she had found someone who would understand her own craving. They would exchange their needs; one need for another. She would provide remedies (and something more besides) for the cramps and the nausea and the fear of what was coming; she, the younger woman, would give her, Charis, who had left it all too late, the baby when she was born. Charis knew it was a girl: she used a herbal diagnostic from Trotula's famous book of recipes.

So when Daisy asked to meet her nonna, Bella thought of Charis on the one hand and of the nameless mother on the other, and both of them haunted her day and night.

As Bella combed her daughter's hair before she put her to bed, maybe Daisy felt the lost mothers through her fingertips and was beginning to hum along to Bella's inward tune, amplifying her nascent yearnings in reciprocal exchange with her, and a song swelled up between them, about the rift in the past and a way to heal it.

Bella began to make enquiries, moving through thickets, struggling over hurdles. When Daisy first declared loudly and firmly that she was looking for her grandmother, the official in the United States consular office in Milan, whom she and Bella went to consult, assumed Bella must be searching for her birth mother. Bella realised the mistake and almost immediately understood that Daisy had divined her own curiosity, her own longing to fill the vacancy.

She was terrified but excited. Daisy was enraptured at the thought: they would find Bella's real mother and she would have a nonna of her own.

The process was complicated because they were now resident in Italy. But after toiling up mountains of documents, after a DNA test and paying out several expensive search fees to lawyers in America, a letter came with a name, an address – in Danville, California – and a photograph, a kind of mug shot, taken before Bella's birth, in which Bella saw nobody she knew or resembled: a thin-faced girl with a mutinous mouth and a back-combed bob, who could have been thirty years old, not the mere eighteen the certificate declared.

It was looking at her mother's face that made Bella decide she must see Charis, too. The two women's meeting in that time before she was born and at the moment of her birth bound them together for ever in the same story, and the story was theirs and couldn't be split in two.

Her resolve formed inside her like a flame; she felt her heart kindle and soar.

The blaze of her realisation gave her the force she needed to inform Piero and warn him that he could not oppose her in this enterprise.

'I am going to New York to see Charis again,' she said. 'It's been long enough.'

He struggled against her; he poured vitriol on Charis. But he was passing his hands over his eyes, as if trying to rub out what he saw there at the same time as he summoned up all the rancour of his memories. And so, beneath all the sound and fury, quietness set in, and Bella understood with a lurch that he would not stop her going.

Not that she would have let him stop her, not now.

So she ran to Daisy's room and scooped her up and cried out to her child, 'How much do I love you?' She was running from one side of the room to the other and all the way round and round – 'Like this, like this!' – as Daisy jumped up and down, howling with laughter. 'And you're going to meet your nonna. We're going to find her.'

She had not dared admit to Piero that she was searching for the other mother in her story, not Charis, not the one he knew, but the one with no name, the one who had given birth to her and then given her away.

She did not show him the copies of the documents she had procured, nor the tickets from New York to San Francisco that she had bought for herself and Daisy; she hid them in a wallet tucked it into its inside pocket, and then thrust the whole thing deep down in the zipped-up lining of her suitcase, a part she never usually used.

She didn't tell Daisy either, not yet. It would depend on what happened when they reached Danville.

Scenes of their reunion danced in a frenzy before her eyes as she tried out the woman in the photograph in different settings:

– they would arrive at the door of a small house with a garden path, crazy paving, and a smoking chimney, and a street lantern haloed to one side. Bella and Daisy would skip towards her, hand in hand ... There would be shock, astonishment, then bliss, bliss, bliss as they would fall into one another's arms –

Or – she was opening doors in the possible time ahead, doors with different scenes behind them – they would find the house empty because, yes, her mother, her real mother, would be at work. So they would knock at a neighbour's door and then go to another address, in downtown Danville, a shop or a bank or a business where she would be working, and they would wait in line for an appointment and then –

The same, the recognition that filled the heart to bursting.

Or:

– she would be living in squalor, in a doss-house, with drunken companions, a school of alkies falling among the debris of empty cans and bottles and roach-ends or worse – needles, carbonised spoons, aluminium foil singed with smoke.

Bella would save her. She would appear in a glow at the door – Daisy would be sheathed in golden light, too. Together, they'd beam out love and warmth, cherishing and nourishing, and the years of separation would dissolve. The discovery of Daisy's existence would bring her hope and a reason to live. They would help her into rehab; they would bring her home with them.

In every one of these scenes, Bella saw her own face slipping to eclipse the features of the woman in the photograph; she found she could not envisage her mother as she might have grown over the last twenty-seven years. She tried greying the dark hair of the woman in the picture; she tried adding lines around her mouth; she tried bowing her shoulders and tensing her neck till it turned scrawny.

The images tumbled through her mind as the plane crossed the world and Daisy fell asleep beside her in her seat, her furry lamb held close to her cheek, which lay against her mother's arm.

Across the cloud floor stretched Bella's dreams of their homecoming: her mother restored to them both, and she, Bella, restored to her – the dream was warm as a soft, sweet pudding straight from the oven, toasted sugar seeping from its fluffy edges; it was thrilling and made her tingle, creeping deliciously over her scalp and down her arms, like the times when Charis used to brush her hair before tucking her up and sometimes tease her by blowing softly on her neck and on her cheeks.

No, she told herself, don't think of her, don't think of Charis.

Bella began to doze, but uneasily. The encounter that lay

ahead loomed, tall as a tall tower before them, a tower difficult to enter and hard to scale, a tower with no doors or windows.

They are driving along the freeway towards the address the bureau has given her after she sent them a sample of her DNA and proved she was who she was when she was born. The GPS map in the hired car is guiding them in a soft, motherly voice:

'You are coming up to the exit. Two hundred yards, one hundred yards. Take the slipway. Take the next left, two hundred yards, one hundred yards.'

The twists and turns continue; they are advancing deeper and deeper into the countryside without a sign of human habitation. On all sides of them the land sweeps up to the horizon in a thick, rough pelt of shrub and undergrowth, bristling, thorny; on the crest of the hills the pine trees stand serried, pointing blades into the cloud cover.

The gentle, persuasive voice keeps directing them. They keep following her instructions, turning, turning again.

Thank God for these systems, Bella thinks. She would never have been able to map-read her way to this place.

Now they are driving into the forest itself on the ridge; the light hangs in limp rags through the lattice of the pines. She can't hear them from inside the car with the AC on but she knows they are soughing. She turns on her headlights, even though it is still daytime.

Daisy begins to stir; Bella realises she doesn't want her to wake up and see what they are driving through, that she is not a little scared herself.

Then a sign appears by the side of the road; the name of the house in the address she has from the bureau comes into focus.

There is an intercom on the gate, angled down towards the driver's window. She presses the buzzer and realises it is mounted with a camera, into whose convex eye she stares, trying to smooth her face into pleasantness.

'Who is it?' says a voice, the sort of voice women used to have when they'd smoked all their lives.

Gripes twist Bella's stomach. She does not recognise that voice. Yet she knows it.

'Mum,' yells Daisy all of a sudden. 'Mum, where are we?'

'I've come to see you. It's been a long time,' begins Bella into the intercom.

'I don't know you,' says the voice. 'Come nearer the camera. Intruders aren't welcome here.'

Daisy snuffles, twists anxiously; after an interval, the electronic arm of the gate slowly rises with a low whirr.

Bella murmurs to her reassuringly, 'We're here. We've arrived – at your nonna's.'

They drive over the rumble of a cattle grid and into a twisting side road, fringed with the same dense ranks of dark trees. The light has drained to a lemon tinge in the afternoon sky.

At the end of the road they can now see the house: a house in the woods, encircled with a palisade, and in the doorway, a tall figure silhouetted against the room behind, holding a torch with the beam pointed towards them.

Bella takes Daisy tightly by the hand and walks toward the house, following the slice of light the beam cuts into the path.

ACKNOWLEDGEMENTS

My profound thanks to Philip Terry, Julia Bell, and Sue Tyley for reading these stories and commenting most helpfully (as well as encouragingly); to Nicholas Royle, at Salt, for taking them on, and to Chris and Jen Hamilton-Emery for publishing the book; to Beatrice Dillon for all her support and thoughtfulness; to Liz Kuti and Adrian May for their encouragement and interest; to Charles Glass, who recommended to me *Wilfrid Blunt's Egyptian Garden: Fox-hunting in Cairo* (London: Stationery Office, 1999), which inspired 'The Family Friend', and to the late Alan Howard who performed the story on the radio; to my family, Conrad and Carolina, and Graeme with my love, always.

I would also like to thank all the editors, who asked me to contribute to their magazines, collections, radio series and other forms of publication, as follows:

'Out of the Burning House', first broadcast on BBC Radio 4, 2004.

'Mélusine: A Mermaid Tale', first published (in French translation) in *Marie-Claude de Brunhoff: Les Théatres immobiles, ed. René de Ceccatty* (Paris: Seuil, 2008).

'Brigit's Cell', first broadcast as 'Birgitta's Cell' on BBC Radio 4, in series 'I Want to Be Alone', 2005.

'A Chatelaine in the Making', first published as 'The Isle of Lanterns; Or, The Young Man in the Gondola of the Air Balloon (After Hoffmann's *Nutcracker Suite*)', *Harper's Bazaar,* December 2010.

'Red Lightning', written for The Art Fund's campaign for the Staffordshire Hoard, first published in *Art Quarterly*, Autumn 2010.

'Watermark', original to this collection, prompted by an invitation from Michel Jeanneret, for which many thanks.

'The Family Friend', written for *Alan Howard Reads* on BBC Radio 4, first broadcast 2007.

'Worm Wrangling', first published in *Heat*, ed. Ivor Indyk (Sydney: 2003).

'After the Fox', first published in *Don't Know a Good Thing: The Asham Award Short-Story Collection*, ed. Kate Pullinger (London, Bloomsbury, 2006).

'Ladybird, Ladybird', first published in *Harper's Bazaar,* December 2005.

'Item, One Tortoiseshell Bag', first published in *AnOther Magazine*, Issue 27, Autumn/Winter 2014.

'Letter to the Unknown Soldier', first published online at www.1418now.org.uk, ed. Kate Pullinger and Neil Bartlett, 2014.

'Forget My Fate', first published in *Midsummer Nights*, ed. Jeanette Winterson, 2009.

'Dolorosa', first published in 'Cadavre exquis (for Aura Satz)', for her exhibition, 2006.

'See No Evil', first published in *Short Fiction*, ed. Anthony Caleshu, Issue 4, 2010.

'Mink', first broadcast in series *Feminine Mystique* BBC Radio 4, 2013.

'A Rare Visit', first published online at http://1001.net.au/story/519, performed by Barbara Campbell, 2006.

'Sing For Me', original to this collection reworked from version, first broadcast as 'Solitudinem faciunt, pacem appellant', in *From Fact to Fiction*, BBC Radio 4, 20 June 2010.

'Breadcrumbs', first published online at http://1001.net.au/story/206 as 'At Night through a Gap', performed by Barbara Campbell, 2006.

'The Difference in the Dose', performed at Bath Music Festival with the Royal College of Art, Bath, 2009, first published in *Marvels & Tales: Journal of Fairy-Tale Studies*, Vol 24, no.2, (2010).

NEW FICTION FROM SALT

RON BUTLIN
Ghost Moon (978-1-907773-77-8)

KERRY HADLEY-PRYCE
The Black Country (978-1-78463-034-8)

IAN PARKINSON
The Beginning of the End (978-1-78463-026-3)

CHRISTOPHER PRENDERGAST
Septembers (978-1-907773-78-5)

JONATHAN TAYLOR
Melissa (978-1-78463-035-5)

GUY WARE
The Fat of Fed Beasts (978-1-78463-024-9)

MEIKE ZIERVOGEL
Kauther (978-1-78463-029-4)

MORE SHORT STORIES FROM SALT

ELIZABETH BAINES
Used to Be (978-1-78463-036-2)

CARYS DAVIES
The Redemption of Galen Pike (978-1-907773-71-6)

STELLA DUFFY
Everything is Moving, Everything is Joined:
The Selected Stories of Stella Duffy (978-1-907773-05-1)

CATHERINE EISNER
A Bad Case and Other Adventures of Disturbed Minds
(978-1-84471-962-4)

MATTHEW LICHT
Justine, Joe and the Zen Garbageman (978-1-84471-829-0)

KIRSTY LOGAN
The Rental Heart and Other Fairytales (978-1-907773-75-4)

DAN POWELL
Looking Out Of Broken Windows (978-1-907773-73-0)

BEST BRITISH SHORT STORIES

Best British Short Stories 2011 (978-1-907773-12-9),
edited by Nicholas Royle

Best British Short Stories 2012 (978-1-907773-18-1),
edited by Nicholas Royle

Best British Short Stories 2013 (978-1-907773-47-1),
edited by Nicholas Royle

Best British Short Stories 2014 (978-1-907773-67-9),
edited by Nicholas Royle

Best British Short Stories 2015 (978-1-78463-027-0),
edited by Nicholas Royle